Before

We

Go

Before

We

Go

AMY BRIGHT

Red Deer Press

Published by Red Deer Press
A Fitzhenry & Whiteside Company
195 Allstate Parkway, Markham
ON, L3R 4T8
www.reddeerpress.com

Edited for the Press by Kathy Stinson
Cover and text design by Daniel Choi
Cover image courtesy Shutterstock

Printed and bound in Canada by Webcom
We acknowledge with thanks the Canada Council for the Arts, and the Ontario Arts Council for their support of our publishing program. We acknowledge the financial support of the Government of Canada through the Canada Book Fund (CBF) for our publishing activities.

 Canada Council for the Arts Conseil des Arts du Canada   ONTARIO ARTS COUNCIL CONSEIL DES ARTS DE L'ONTARIO

Library and Archives Canada Cataloguing in Publication
Bright, Amy
Before we go / Amy Bright.
ISBN 978-0-88995-471-7
I. Title.

PS8603.R542B43 2012   jC813ʹ.6   C2012-901853-8

Publisher Cataloging-in-Publication Data (U.S)
Bright, Amy.
Before we go / Amy Bright.
[240] p. : cm.
Summary: When 17-year-old Emily visits her dying grandmother in hospital, she meets teen-aged Alex and his sister. The three kids are propelled toward a surprising future by family secrets that have spanned generations.
ISBN: 978-0-88995-471-7 (pbk.)
1. Teenagers and death – Juvenile fiction. I. Title.
[Fic] dc23   PZ7.B7548Be 2012

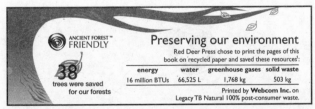

ANCIENT FOREST™ FRIENDLY

Preserving our environment
Red Deer Press chose to print the pages of this book on recycled paper and saved these resources[1]:

	energy	water	greenhouse gases	solid waste
38 trees were saved for our forests	16 million BTUs	66,525 L	1,768 kg	503 kg

Printed by Webcom Inc. on
Legacy TB Natural 100% post-consumer waste.

[1]Estimates were made using the Environmental Defense Paper Calculator.

FSC
www.fsc.org
MIX
Paper from
responsible source
FSC® C00407

For my sister Erin

chapter*one*

Emily wondered when she would start feeling the way they told her she would. She was holding a binder full of papers open on her lap, pages typed up neatly by nurses and doctors that outlined acceptable reactions for everything. They had titles like, "How to Deal with the Death of a Loved One" and "Is There Life After Death?" They were a set of instructions for how she was supposed to react to the fact that her grandmother was dying.

Most of the papers were part of thick information packets, stapled neatly together at the top left corner. The others were as brief as a single page, a bulleted listing embellished by flowered borders and colorless clip-art. They were supposed to be a reminder of how to get from point A to point B, directions, because she wasn't supposed to know the way. But all of them, Emily noticed, were missing the information she wanted most: the way back, back to before brochures, waiting rooms, and tight, straightened smiles.

"Kate?"

Emily quickly shoved the binder, the papers furtively tucked inside, into her backpack.

"It's me, Grandma," she said. "Emily. Mom's not here."

"Did you just get here?" Emily's grandmother asked. There was a crease between her eyebrows that smoothed out when she smiled. She coughed a few times, and Emily waited until she had finished to answer.

"A little while ago," Emily said. She had taken the bus to the hospital just after dinner. She had been sitting beside the bed for fifteen minutes with the papers from Dr. Lanagan, waiting for her grandmother to wake up.

"It's New Year's Eve," her grandmother said.

"Yeah."

"Are you going out tonight?"

"I'm going to stay here with you. Remember?"

Emily stroked out a wrinkle that had built in the sheets. Her heart beat a circle in her chest and she tried to make it still.

"I don't want you staying here all night."

"But I want to."

What she meant was *but I have to*.

Her grandmother gave a small shake of her head, like a twitch, an involuntary movement. She held her hand to her chest and swallowed back a fit of coughing that Emily knew would escape again before long.

"I'm staying," Emily repeated.

The hospital room was so bare that Emily felt like she was sitting in little more than a boxed-off space. The time she had spent here over the past few weeks blurred from distinct days into indistinct hours, almost like it wasn't happening to her at all.

There was a square metal table beside the hospital bed, the legs ending in wheels. Emily looked at the picture balanced on top of the table. Three faces were tucked carefully inside a frame: Emily, her grandmother, and her grandfather. The photo had been taken in the backyard of her grandparent's house the year before. Her grandfather had propped up the camera on a tripod and set it on a self-timer. There was no one behind the camera. It was only the three of them.

And now, here in the small room at the Victoria General Hospital, there were only two of them, Emily and her grandmother.

"I didn't know you brought this with you," Emily said.

She touched the corner of the glass, where her face was, and covered it behind her thumb. Emily wondered what it would have been like if her mom hadn't sent her to live with her grandparents, if it had just been her grandmother and grandfather in that big house together. Emily wouldn't have taken the bedroom on the second floor, or claimed the long kitchen table for homework. She took her hand away from the picture frame, leaving behind a fingerprint on the glass. She cleaned it off with the sleeve of her sweater.

Footsteps sounded from down the hall and slid into the silence of the room. Angela, one of the nurses at the hospital, appeared at the door. Her clipboard knocked against the outside of her thigh.

"Hi Emily," Angela said.

"Hi," Emily said.

"How are you feeling today, Mrs. Henderson?"

Emily's grandmother gave the sort of shrug that left a wide gap between her collarbone and hospital gown.

Angela moved quickly around the room and Emily pushed her chair backwards and sideways to stay out of the way. When Angela was finished, she stood back from the bed. Her hands wrapped tightly around one another.

"Are you sure you don't want me to bring up a TV for tonight? See the ball drop in New York and everything?"

"No," Emily's grandmother said. "I'm fine."

Emily knew her grandmother didn't want a reminder of the New Year. That she was leaving behind one year for another didn't make her happy or excited. She didn't have a list of resolutions to scribble down on paper or a tremendous belief that *this year would be different*. The last day of the year was just another ending.

"Are you going out tonight?" Emily asked Angela.

Emily picked at the cuticle of her thumb with her index finger, carefully, so that it didn't tear open.

"Can't," Angela said, tapping her clipboard. "I'm working. Are you?"

"I'm staying here tonight," Emily said.

Angela looked at her curiously.

"Emily, I'm sorry. Visiting hours end at seven."

"It's just me," Emily said. "It's not like there's tons of people in here."

"I can't. I'm sorry."

"It's okay, Emily," her grandmother said. "I'm getting tired. There wouldn't be anything for you to do even if you did stay here."

"But that's okay," Emily said.

Arguing in front of Angela was something she tried to avoid. She stood there like someone who was not quite a stranger and not quite a friend. Emily knew Angela listened, even when her eyes slid down to look at the linoleum floor as she pretended not to.

"Not tonight," her grandmother repeated.

"I'll be back around seven, okay Emily?" Angela said.

When Emily didn't answer, Angela left the room. Her flat shoes made squeaking noises as they moved across the linoleum floor, as if they were still damp from the winter wet. It had rained all afternoon.

"When she comes back, you go with her."

"Where?" Emily asked.

Her grandmother didn't answer.

Eventually they resettled into the silence. Emily moved

her chair close to the bed again and her grandmother slid back under the covers. They didn't say anything more to one another. Emily turned the pages of a magazine without really reading the words. While she did that, her grandmother fell asleep. Emily noticed the easy way her grandmother's eyes were concluded by wrinkles, sinking into lines that had been there for as long as Emily could remember.

Emily's grandmother had been in the hospital for just over a month. Emily had driven her to the hospital in the middle of November, just after Remembrance Day, and parked her grandmother's small white car on the street. Overnight, fall had turned into winter. The day before, the trees were flushed with red, orange, yellow, and gold leaves. But when Emily stepped out of the car, she saw that they lay on the damp and sodden sidewalk, drowning in gutters filled with rainwater and mud. Emily and her grandmother had to step gingerly over the broken branches on the cement. Her grandmother's walker stuttered over the debris left from the night before.

"Must've been some storm," her grandmother said.

Emily hadn't slept the night before she took her grandmother to the hospital. She lay awake in her bedroom on the top floor of her grandmother's house, watching the hyphenated numbers on her bedside clock cycle through late night to early morning. The wind shook the windows, bouncing the skinny screen against the glass pane. The curtains in Emily's room fluttered where the cracks that ran along the four sides of the windows let the wind in. They billowed inward every few minutes, leaving a ghostly, person-sized impression, between the window and the room. Emily lay still in her bed when the thunder started. It wasn't the rumbling sound that came in intervals between flashes of lightning, the count-to-six-and-the-storm-is-six-miles-away thunder. It was a dangerous undercurrent of sound that crouched above the house and groaned. Down the street, Emily knew everyone in Veronica's house would be sitting in the living room together, listening to the storm. The storms that came in the middle of the night and tumbled down, rollicking summersaults of sound that bent downwards, were the ones that kept Emily paralyzed. Meanwhile, her best friend Veronica's family went down into the living room, opened up the blinds and the curtains, and watched the storm as it rose to the height of wind and rain. In the house Emily lived in with her grandmother, there was no one else to meet downstairs at two in the morning. It was Emily in her room and her grandmother across the hall, both with blankets and sheets tucked tightly into the corners in the military way that it had been done in the house for years. That's what Emily's mom had told her. "Your grandmother, she lashed down the sheets every morning, and every night I'd lie there trapped and unmoving, knowing it was part of her plan."

"What plan?" Emily had asked.

"To keep me away from the boys," her mom said, winking with her left eye. She always winked with the same eye, blinking it closed with a conspiratorial nod.

Emily didn't understand what it meant, even though she went through the habit of discussing the bed sheets with her mom every time she came to the island for a visit. They'd go through the pattern of the repeating conversation without moving any further past what they had rehearsed every time before. Emily had never asked, "What boys?" even though she was sure one of them had to have been her father.

But that night, with the thunder directly overhead, Emily climbed out of bed, her feet finding the folds where the sheets hugged the mattress, and crept downstairs. Her grandmother's door had been closed, without any light seeping out under the crack at the bottom of the door. Her grandmother had eaten dinner, her last meal before she began the twelve-hour fast for her surgery the next day, where she'd be getting a new hip to replace what she called her "bum old one." Emily turned on the light above the oven and poured a glass of water from the tap. The blinds were all shut tight, but she could hear the steady trickle of water running down the outside of the glass windows, dripping in long rivulets that fell into the yard at the back of the house. Emily pulled at the cord to open the blinds. She couldn't see anything. Where she lived with her grandmother was dark at night, with streetlights positioned under the tall trees and high hedges that drained the light before it reached the ground.

Emily had this feeling about tomorrow, the day she would drive her grandmother to the hospital. When she was eleven, Emily's grandparents packed up her duffel bag, her sleeping bag, and a pillow into the back of the car to take her up-island to camp. Emily had felt an overwhelming desire to trade places with her grandparents. For them, the trip was just a drive. A couple of hours there, a couple of hours back. For Emily, it was being left on her own for a week. It was people she didn't know and square cabins and bunk beds and communal bathrooms. It was meals that were set at precise and unwavering times and rhymes and songs sung and skits that she'd have to act in like she knew the punch line they were moving toward. It was staying awake all night and it was wishing time would go faster, and it was wanting to be home.

In the morning, Emily would be driving her grandmother to the hospital. It was a drive there and a drive back. It was a sandwich in the cafeteria. It was sitting in her grandmother's room at the end of it and holding her hand and figuring out her medication so they could go home. It wasn't Emily's turn to be dropped off in a strange place. She was on the other side of that.

She sat in the kitchen until the storm passed over the house. The rain stopped and its absence was something she missed, the consistent sound of background noise that neither Emily nor her grandmother knew how to add to the house. The sun didn't come up in the morning. The grey sky just shifted beneath the fog, running through the limited spectrum of stormy color. Quiet on the stairs, Emily went back to her bedroom. She found a pair of jeans on top of her laundry basket, clean enough to wear for another day. She opened her dresser drawers, her clothes unfolded and sloppy. There was a wrinkled shirt with long sleeves that she sprayed with perfume and pulled on overtop of a T-shirt. She sat on her bed and waited until her grandmother woke up and knocked on her door to tell her it was time to go.

"I just wonder if we'll need to get the roof redone. If it's going to be another winter like last year with all that rain. You're not getting any leaking in your bedroom, are you?" Emily's grandmother asked her as they turned the corner and neared the hospital doors. Emily steadied the metal walker. The wheels launched over a fallen branch, twigs forking into a slingshot shape.

"You okay?" Emily asked her.

"You'd think they'd have someone out here taking care of this mess," her grandmother said. "I'm going to need a double hip surgery by the time we get there."

Emily smiled and navigated them to the front doors of the hospital. She kicked away the larger pieces of leaves and tree that had fallen on the sidewalk. Once they were inside, Emily talked to the receptionist, found her grandmother's room number, and took them up in the elevator.

"So, what are we going to do to celebrate," Emily asked her as the floors went up, "when you're out of the hospital?"

"I don't know, Emily," she said, sighing. "It's going to take a lot of time to recover. But maybe we'll be able to do something when this is over."

There were yellow leaves stuck on the underside of the walker. They were slick with rain and were dirty from the sidewalk. Emily didn't move to unpeel the leaves from the wheels in the elevator.

"Maybe we'll just order something for dinner," Emily said. "We can start with that."

"We'll start with that," her grandmother repeated.

Emily stayed in the room just long enough to watch the nurses prep her grandmother for surgery. She left her grandmother's purse in the cupboard with a duffel bag that contained several sweaters and a couple of books. She leaned over the bed and kissed her grandmother on the forehead. Emily felt her grandmother squeeze her hand.

"I'll see you in a couple of hours," Emily said.

"Don't stick around here all day," her grandmother said. "I'm not going anywhere."

"Me neither."

She went downstairs to the cafeteria. She hadn't eaten breakfast that morning. She didn't want to eat anything in front of her grandmother, who couldn't eat anything, whose stomach was probably nervously flipping around in anticipation of what was to come. Emily took a tray off the top of a stack of similar ones and rolled it down the metal countertop. She picked up a yogurt, a banana, and a chocolate chip muffin. There was a refrigerator with rows and rows of drinks and she grabbed a juice off the top shelf. She took her tray to a table by the window and sat down.

Emily's mom should have been with her at the hospital, especially since it was *her* mother who was having surgery. They were three generations stacked one after the other, except Emily's mother was always missing from that middle space. At least this time it wasn't last minute when her mom had decided not to come. She'd called a week before the surgery, talking to Emily first and then to Emily's grandmother.

"Honey, something's come up," she said, like she always said. "I don't think I can make it."

"You're not coming for the surgery?"

"I can't."

"That's pretty shitty, Mom."

"I'll be there after. I just can't come until the weekend. I'll be around while she's recovering."

"Mom," Emily said, but her mom leaped forward to something else.

"So how's school doing? Everything okay?" She pushed the two separate topics together as if it was natural that they should follow one another.

"It's fine. It's school, Mom. It's high school."

"You're so smart, Em. You're not like I was in high school. I didn't have any motivation. I'd get these terrible marks and not even care."

"Yeah, yeah," Emily said. Their conversations were the same. They looped without change. "How's Vancouver?"

"Oh, it's the same as always," her mom said. "Rain, rain, rain. We use it all up here before it can cross the ocean to get to you."

"It's been raining here, too."

The rain in Victoria would hang like curtains. Emily's mom had an apartment in Vancouver with strings of beads that hung from the doorframes. The skinny strings and plastic beads slipped over Emily's shoulders when she walked under them the same way the rain danced and dripped in Victoria.

"Em, honey, we're okay, right? You and me? Everything's okay between us."

"It's fine, Mom."

"It doesn't seem fine."

"It is."

When Emily said things differently, when she said, "No, it's not fine. I hate that you're not here and I hate that you're not going to be back on the island for Grandma's surgery," her mom would get very silent on the other end of the phone. They would say goodbye and Emily would hand the phone off to her grandmother, and she'd listen to their conversation from the living room, thinking it was good and kind and normal. But then a week later, when her mom would call to check in on things, the phone would hang on the wall in silence. Emily might as well turn off her cell phone. Her mom wouldn't be calling.

It would go on like that until something important happened in Vancouver. Her mom would get a good story to write for the newspaper or she'd be sent across the country to cover something national. Then the phone would ring and she'd be excited and animated, with her voice staying in a high octave that Emily associated with her mom being as far away as possible from Victoria, from Emily, and from Emily's grandmother.

Emily ate breakfast in the cafeteria while her grandmother was in surgery. She set her cell phone on the table and considered calling her mom, just to manufacture a way out of the loneliness. She had three hours to fill before her grandmother would be out of the operating room, out of recovery, and back in her room.

The sky had cleared by the time she went outside. The car was still parked where she'd left it, and a few leaves had fallen from the tree and were stuck in between the windshield and the windshield wipers. They were mostly yellow and dirty, muddied, even though she couldn't see how they had found their way to the ground. She dug them out of the mirror with her shirtsleeve covering her hand and got into the car.

Emily pulled away from the hospital and drove to the

movie theaters downtown. There were six movies playing. She picked one of them, the one that had the right start time, and went inside the dark theater.

Emily sat at the back and felt time stop while she was in the theater. She didn't have to count down minutes or hours. While her grandmother was on an operating table getting a new hip on the other side of the city, Emily sat in the darkness of the theater and watched things happen to other people. At the end of the movie, she drove back to the hospital.

Now it was New Year's Eve, and several weeks had passed since that trip downtown. Emily shook her head, trying not to think of the things that had changed. When the room became as quiet as it would get, even with the ticking and beeping of the machines behind her, Emily reached beneath her chair. She opened her binder and unfolded the papers.

Her grandmother was not going to leave this hospital. And somewhere at the bottom of the paper was written an "acceptance" that was easier to read about than it was to do.

chapter*two*

Alex stood in front of the full-length mirror that hung from the back of the door. The door was closed to the hallway, where he could hear the shuffle of footsteps and the roll of plastic wheels on the floor.

He had already made up the small bed by the window. He did it the way he did at home, when he threw the top sheet over everything else. His bed-making technique always made his mom yell at him to make it neater, or to pull the sheets tighter, or to smooth down the wrinkles. But here, he didn't need it to be perfect.

Alex's jeans were loose on his legs. He held them up with a brown belt, cinched to the last optional hole. He was wearing a striped sweater and a heavy winter jacket. His shoes were tied, the bottoms crusted with mud from the last time he had worn them. *Almost two weeks ago*, Alex thought. *I haven't worn shoes in almost two weeks.*

"Okay," he said, nodding at himself in the mirror. "Okay."

His cell phone rang on the side table by the bed. He crossed the room to retrieve it, saw his sister's name on the caller ID, and picked it up.

"Hey, Lucy," he said.

"Did you get all of your stuff?" Her voice was muffled and quiet, different from her usual sixteen-year-old way of talking. Alex wondered where she was calling from, knowing only that it would be somewhere away from their parents.

"I got it. Thanks for the belt."

"You're so skinny," she said, concerned.

"I'm okay."

"Alex," Lucy said. "We don't have to do this."

"Yes, we do." They had gone over their plan so many times that Alex could recite it from memory.

"There are other ways we can tell her. We can do it right here. You don't even have to leave."

"This is the way I want it to be. Please."

Alex tucked his wallet into his back pocket. It held some cash from Christmas, a couple of twenty-dollar bills from his parents.

"I think I should go," Alex said, looking up at the clock. "It's almost time. You'll meet me in half an hour?"

"I'll be there," Lucy said.

Alex ended the call. His hands were shaking. He held them out in front of him and watched them twitch, his fingers dancing a stuttered pattern in the air. He stuffed them, along with his cell phone, into his pockets. The weight of the phone was reassuring against his thigh.

There wasn't anything more that he could do. He took one more look around the room. The curtains were open to the darkness outside. He let them fall shut. The bathroom door was closed and everything was straight, neat, and orderly. Alex held onto the inside pockets of his jeans with his hands. Finally, they became still.

He opened the door and walked into the hall.

chapter*three*

Angela had made it clear that when visiting hours were over, Emily would have to leave. Even though this was her routine now—school, hospital, home—she still always hesitated before returning to her grandmother's house. At least at the hospital, there were people around.

Emily didn't wait for Angela to come back before leaving her grandmother's room. She filled the glass of water on the bedside table, adjusted the lamp, and smoothed down the sheets. She walked down the white-walled hallways toward the elevator.

The intercom buzzed, the wheels of trolleys rolled along the floor, nurses and doctors talked in low and urgent voices. Emily wanted to record the noise on her phone, take it home, and play it in the empty house, like a prescription for dealing with being lonely.

Visitors trickled from open doorways, mostly in twos

and threes, shoulders touching and arms close. Emily trailed along behind them and stepped into the crowded elevator after everyone else. She squished herself against the front wall. It was stuffy and close, the soggy smell of winter on jackets.

Someone tapped Emily on the shoulder. That deliberate tap was especially unexpected in the elevator, where her shoulders already touched other shoulders and chests and elbows.

"I think you're on my foot," said a voice behind her.

Emily had to move her head very carefully in order to look down at the pair of black and white sneakers. She blushed and her neck went hot.

"Sorry," she said, and, even though she wasn't sure if she had been standing on the shoes, adjusted her feet and stared at the closed metal doors of the elevator.

"You were all lopsided," the voice said. "It looked uncomfortable."

Emily turned around. Behind her stood a tall boy with messy hair. Emily stared first at the hair before she looked at his face, pale and careful and thoughtful.

"Thanks."

Other people looked in their direction, the only two speaking in the elevator. Here, eavesdropping could just be listening.

"It's pretty crowded in here," he continued.

"It's not that bad."

"You're used to crowded places?"

"No," Emily said. "Not really."

"I am," the boy said. "You know what they're doing at my high school?" Emily shook her head. "They want to build more classrooms, because it's overcrowded. But it's not overcrowded enough for them to start construction. So they pushed us all together into this one wing of the school to show that we really need help."

The elevator stopped on the next floor. A few people got out, and even more filed in.

"What school do you go to?" she asked.

"Churchill High School."

"Yeah, I guess I heard about that," Emily said.

"You can't even move your elbows in the hallways," the boy said.

He moved his arms as if to show her, and his elbow met with the side of the man standing beside him. The man's face wrinkled at the unexpected elbow to his ribs. Emily tried not to laugh.

"So what I'm saying is that it's busy tonight," the boy said. "And kind of like my high school."

"Well, it's New Year's," Emily said.

"Were you here at Christmas? Christmas seemed busier."

Christmas at the hospital, Emily remembered, had been packed. In the morning, small, plastic Christmas trees were lugged up to rooms, balanced between boxes packed with wrapped presents, tins of cookies, and mugs filled with coffee. By early afternoon torn wrapping paper overflowed in garbage bins, sliding along the floor in long, snaking ribbons.

Emily had brought her grandmother a carton of eggnog and a packet of gingerbread on Christmas morning. Angela told her she wasn't allowed to give her grandmother either. Not the unpasteurized eggs in the eggnog or the cookies made with things that were on one of Angela's lists, right beneath a stern red x. On her way out, Emily took both back to the lobby and dropped them in the trashcan, almost missing the bin because she was so angry.

"Yeah, I was here at Christmas."

She watched the floors ticking down from 4 to 3 to 2, her shoulders loosening with the anticipation of the conversation ending.

"You have to be a regular to be here for the holidays."

"I guess."

"So you're here often?"

"Every day." She paused. "Are you?"

"All the time," he answered.

The doors opened and Emily pushed around the corner of the elevator and into the atrium.

It wasn't until she was halfway to the front doors that she noticed two feet moving beside her, feet in beat-up black and white sneakers, walking in the same direction as she was.

"Do you have a friend in here?" the boy asked, matching her pace.

"My grandma. What about you?"

"Intensive care," he said, shrugging. "Cancer."

"Oh. I'm sorry."

"So am I."

The boy pushed open the front doors; Emily had to duck under his arm while he held it awkwardly open for her. The cold settled into her teeth and nostrils, the tips of her ears, and the back of her throat. Emily and the boy stopped at the end of the cement sidewalk, beside a row of benches and a garbage can.

"I'm Alex, by the way," the boy said. The way he said his name was like shoulders lifting in a shrug.

"Emily."

"Sorry for bothering you in the elevator," he said.

"It's okay."

"You looked like you needed someone to talk to. And you were also on my foot."

Emily's laugh came out of her nose more than her mouth.

"No, I wasn't," she said. She wiggled her fingers in the palms of her mittens and shoved her hands into her pockets. Alex noticed.

"It's cold," Emily said.

"It's winter."

"I wish we had snow instead of cold rain."

"No can do in the Pacific Northwest. Not with the ocean,"

Alex said, looking toward the coast.

"Still," Emily said, rubbing her hands together. "I wish it would snow."

Alex watched her and she felt her lips tingling in the damp air. Sometimes the cold made her words come out wrong, like they were frozen in place before they could get out of her mouth.

"Can I ask you something, Emily?"

Emily nodded.

"Are you doing anything for New Year's?"

"No. I thought I'd be able to stay here. With my grandma. Now I guess I'll just go home."

"My sister's coming to pick me up in a half-hour. We're meeting at a fast food place a few blocks away. You want to come and get something to eat?"

There was a buzzing sound coming from behind her ears. Emily hadn't gone out with anyone since her grandmother went to the hospital for the first time. She hadn't invited anyone over to her house, and she hadn't been invited to anyone else's. For almost two months, she had been living in a small, carefully constructed world that she had made for herself.

Since it was New Year's, there were decorations outside the hospital, a big banner with thick, colorful letters spelling out the holiday. Emily's chest contracted at the thought of spending New Year's alone at her grandmother's house.

Alex was stomping his feet on the ground, warming them

up inside his shoes. Emily curled her toes in her boots. She blinked hard.

"Okay," she said. "I'll go with you."

In the quiet cold, Alex's eyes were bright. Emily wrapped her arms around herself, tugged at her jacket, and pulled at her mittens. And then she followed Alex away from the hospital.

chapter*four*

Emily and Alex walked down the sidewalk. They both avoided stepping on the cracks cut into the cement. Emily noticed that the patterned step of Alex's feet lined up with hers and she quickly changed her own, breaking the synchronicity.

"So who were you visiting?" Emily asked.

"A friend," Alex said.

"I'm sorry," Emily said. "It's nice that you go on New Year's."

"Yeah, well, holidays," he said. "I guess they're kind of tough."

He didn't say anything else, even though Emily knew there must be more. She wondered if she had done the right thing, leaving the hospital with Alex. It wasn't that she hadn't wanted to go with him. It was just that she wasn't used to doing things so quickly, letting words come out without even thinking about them.

They crossed the street to the park, Emily just ahead of Alex. She watched the way his feet scuffed against the cement, how his hair stuck up around his ears. She tried to make him familiar through small details. The funny thing was that she didn't have to try very hard. He seemed like someone she had known for longer than she had.

Emily was used to the quiet walk; she did it every day. Out through the double doors of the hospital, down the street, and through the park to the bus stop by the gas station. She liked the bus. She didn't drive her grandmother's car very often. From here, she would usually take one half-hour bus ride to her grandparent's house—her grandmother's house —and soon, she knew, her house. When it happened, when the inevitable end to the pneumonia her grandmother had contracted in the hospital occurred, her mom might move back to Victoria. Emily hoped for that. But it was more likely that she would stay in Vancouver. She might make Emily move. Emily thought about those things in the middle of the night when there was no one she could call and talk to. Walking with someone she didn't even know felt more stable and permanent than what would happen next with her family.

There were lampposts at measured intervals to light the path through the park. Emily could hear voices beside and behind her. New Year's Eve was one of the few nights of the year that she liked being outside late. It seemed like everyone was awake and everyone was out, doing something for the holiday. If she were walking alone, she knew she'd feel excluded and isolated, the only one who wasn't among people. With Alex, she could believe she was at least part of something outside of herself. She might not even know him, but it was enough to be walking with him on New Year's, without plans or expectations for what happened next. Emily needed a break from jumping to the end of things and trying to figure out what would happen there.

They crossed the park and came out on the other side next to a suburban strip mall, its shops huddled together, hugging the cement ground. Emily watched Alex and she felt like he was watching her back, as if through their tiny glances they were composing something like the definition of what it meant to be an Alex or an Emily.

Alex put his hand on the restaurant door and left his fingerprints behind on the damp glass.

"My sister should be here soon," he said.

"What's her name?" Emily tried to picture a family around Alex, but she couldn't quite imagine what a sister would look like.

"Lucy."

"Lucy's a pretty name."

"She doesn't think so. Mom used to make this joke. Instead of saying, 'I love you,' at night, she'd say 'I love Lucy' like the TV show."

"That's not so bad."

They stepped up to the counter. Emily's stomach growled as she waited to order. She tried to remember the last time she had eaten. She had gotten into the habit of grabbing something on the way home from the hospital. Sometimes Angela would bring an extra tray of food for Emily to eat with her grandmother around dinnertime. Emily would eat it gratefully, glad not to have to find something later, but it wasn't often that Angela remembered to bring one for her. Most of the time it was Emily sitting in the chair, watching her grandmother eat from the sections of the tray, the squares and circles that contained the basic meat, vegetable, potato, juice, dessert that came every night. Her grandmother always pushed the dessert toward Emily.

"It's too sweet."

"It's not bad," Emily would say, scooping it with an unused spoon. The food was usually bland and nondescript, but she didn't complain. It wasn't worth it to make food into a big deal, when there were already so many things that she worried about.

Emily looked at the menu. She was overwhelmed by the options. She liked it when things were straightforward and easy, when the correct choice was clear. She looked at the burgers and the sandwiches and the meals and the drinks. She picked at random. She was doing things differently. The routine that had caused her to approach everything in the same, careful way was breaking down.

It didn't feel strange, standing in the restaurant with

someone she had just met. Alex and Emily's shoulders were touching and they could have been friends. They would look like friends to anyone who saw them. And, Emily thought, maybe they already were.

chapter*five*

Lucy did not want to be stealing the car. *Borrowing* the car, she reminded herself. Alex just called it stealing when he wanted to annoy her. She knew this wasn't that. Still, she felt guilty about doing it. Mostly because her parents were going to kill her, but also because she wondered if Alex would continue through with everything if she just didn't show up. She wondered if he would just go back to the hospital and pretend they hadn't planned for the last week how to make this work. By not showing up, she might be able to stop the night from happening. But part of her knew that Alex would just find another way without her, and she didn't want him to do everything alone. She would not let Alex be alone.

Lucy's parents were in the living room watching TV. They put it on when they got home, a nightly ritual of news and sports and sitcoms. They were talking to each other. Lucy stopped by the back door to listen.

"Do you think we could have done more?" Lucy's mom asked. "Do you think we're giving up?"

"We're not giving up," her dad said. "Don't call it that."

"It's the first time we're not doing anything."

"There's nothing else we can do."

"There has to be something."

Lucy placed her hand on the doorknob and turned, muffling the sound with her palm. The garage was freezing. She stepped to the other side of the door and closed it behind her, hoping her parents hadn't noticed the momentary change in temperature.

She had grabbed the car keys after they got back from dinner. She had gone with her parents to a small restaurant in downtown Victoria, where she had shuffled food around on her plate for an hour without eating very much of it. She hated how many questions her parents asked when Alex wasn't around. They were endless. They were about school and the bus and her friends and her homework, and was she doing well on all of her tests. They were rapid-fire and relentless, and Lucy answered them one-worded if she could.

Lucy climbed into the driver's seat. She wanted to make sure she was ready before she opened the garage, which made a creaking, heavy sound that she could sometimes hear from the living room, telling her that someone was home. It was a warning for her to stop whatever she was doing, if it was something that maybe she shouldn't be doing. She put the key in the ignition, and placed her hands on the steering wheel.

"You can do this, you can do this," she said.

She pushed the garage door opener at the same time she turned the ignition. She backed out of the garage and down the driveway. Her parents didn't open the back door. If they noticed the sound, they hadn't come outside to investigate. Lucy clicked the button again and the door closed behind her.

Lucy hadn't learned all of the different driving maneuvers that she knew she had to know for when she took her driving test. She had her learner's license now, which meant she could drive a car whenever she wanted to, as long as there was an adult in the passenger seat picking apart the things she was doing wrong. Her dad was notorious for pumping the nonexistent brakes. Her mom would clutch the plastic bar beside the door handle.

She turned off the radio. The station switched to French at night and Lucy hadn't taken that since grade eight. Lucy reversed down the driveway before putting the car in drive. The old metal van made a grinding sound of resistance.

"Come on, come on," Lucy said. She knew the van was on its last legs, the wheels almost falling off, but she needed it to hold together for one more night. The gears clicked and she pulled out of the neighborhood.

Driving was easy when she was going straight. As soon as a corner came up, Lucy hesitated, panicked, and almost hit the curb. After that, she got onto a street that wound and curved. She eased into the corners, which were easier than the full-on turns that she would get stuck with at the stop-lights and stop signs.

She was almost at the restaurant she had agreed on with Alex when her cell phone started ringing. She had left it in the cup holder in the front seat, the screen facing out so she could read the caller ID without picking up. It was the home phone number. When Lucy didn't answer, her phone started buzzing with text messages. Her parents knew that she read those, even if she didn't answer.

Where are you?

Lucy, come home.

It's illegal for you to drive alone.

And then the one that Lucy hoped she wouldn't get for at least another hour.

Alex is missing. We're going to the hospital.

"Alex," Lucy said under her breath, "I hope you know what you're doing."

Five minutes later, she turned into the parking lot. She pulled her boots up and zipped her jacket to her chin. Her heart was beating fast. She took a deep breath and then she got out of the car.

chapter*six*

Emily and Alex sat in a small white booth next to a wall of windows. The booth was hard and made of stiff, molded plastic, the kind that made Emily want to sit on the edge of her seat to avoid the uncomfortable feeling of plastic inching into her back.

They shared a tray between them, piled high with hamburgers and fries that tumbled onto the paper placemat, splotches of grease pooling around the fallen food. Emily noticed that Alex didn't eat much. She was halfway through the fries before he had even touched his hamburger.

"Not hungry?" she asked, her mouth full.

"I'm a slow eater," he said.

After that, he peeled back all the food wrappers and picked at a little of everything, but Emily could see that most of the food was still left untouched.

"How was your grandmother doing?" Alex said eventually. "When you were visiting."

He was sitting back in the booth, leaning into the hard plastic. Emily dropped two empty packets of ketchup on the tray.

"Not very good," she said. "I really wish I hadn't left her tonight."

"They get strict with visiting hours."

"I just think she gets so lonely. I hate leaving her."

"She might want a little quiet," he said.

"But I'm quiet around her."

"I guess I mean there're different kinds of quiet. The kind you get from people and the kind you get from being by yourself."

"Maybe," Emily said. "I just don't like that she has to be alone."

But it was really about not wanting to be alone herself, even though time was creeping toward a place where alone would be something she would have to figure out. And alone wouldn't mean the hours spent after school in an empty house, or a quiet evening by herself while her grandmother was out at a meeting. That was *quiet*. *This* was the knowledge that no one would be coming home once the silence got too loud.

At the back of her head was the insistence that she was supposed to be remembering something. Someone. She was supposed to remember that, because of her mother, she would not really be completely alone. But she didn't rely on her mother being there. She had learned not to.

"So what's your sister like?" Emily asked, changing the subject to the only one they had shared.

"You'll have to meet her."

"Is she driving you home?"

"I don't know yet. I don't know what we're doing." He paused, his hands bunching up the napkin on the tray. "You should come with us. Me and Lucy. We'll figure out something to do. There's a lot going on."

"I might just go home," Emily said.

"Why?"

Emily couldn't think of a reason why. All week she had been trying to find a way not to go home. The impending New Year's holiday had weighed on her like something that needed to be passed and put behind her. Now, thinking of going home, she was sliding back into routine, as if she didn't know how to change the habitual in and out that she was so used to.

"Come with us," Alex said again.

"I don't know ..."

"It's New Year's," he insisted.

Emily finished eating the fries on the tray and took a sip of Coke. The options were either to go home or go somewhere that she couldn't anticipate or guess at. Alex said he didn't even know where they were going. Emily had gotten used to the pattern of place to place to place. The sudden expectation of having no expectation scared her and excited her all at once. A way out of what her life had turned into.

From outside came the sound of a car engine, rumbling into the parking lot. There was also a lot of clanking and a grinding sound like metal dragging on cement. She looked out through the window and directly into the yellow head-lights of an old blue van. The paint was chipped and the windshield was cracked.

"That's Lucy," Alex said. "Maybe she'll convince you."

A girl jumped out of the van onto the sidewalk. Her legs moved ahead of her, skinny in tight jeans. Her boots went up to her shins, and Emily noticed the girl's scarf untwist from around her neck and tangle around her feet. The girl shook it out and looped it around her wrist, and when she slammed the van door, the entire vehicle shook. Without locking the doors, she pocketed the keys.

Alex seemed like the kind of person Emily could spend the rest of the evening with and not worry about where they were going or what they would do. She didn't know if Lucy would be the same, or the opposite.

Emily watched Lucy walk toward the restaurant. She wasn't dressed up. It was as if she had been sitting on the couch watching TV all night, remembered her brother needed a ride home, and had driven to pick him up.

And as she watched Lucy get closer, Emily thought, *maybe. Maybe I will go with them.*

chapter*seven*

"There's my big brother!" Lucy said.

She slid into the booth next to Alex and wrapped her arm around his shoulder. Emily sank back into the booth, a half-eaten french fry pinched between her fingers. She wondered what it must be like to have someone like that, the built-in safety net that came from being close with family.

"You're late," Alex said.

Lucy pulled away.

"I'm late? Let's just remember what I had to do to get here. Sneak out of the house? Steal the family car? Drive illegally?" She grinned across the table at Emily. "What do you think? That should get me off the hook, right?"

Emily nodded, smiling, but not really understanding. "You stole a car?" she asked.

"I borrowed the car," she said. "I'm Lucy."

Emily wiped the french fry grease off her hand so she could shake Lucy's.

"Emily."

"I met Emily at the hospital," Alex explained. "She got kicked out at the end of visiting hours."

"Aw, that sucks. Happens to us all the time," Lucy said, jerking her thumb toward her brother.

Alex blushed and covered his sister's hand with his own and Emily watched them exchange a look. When they looked at her again, she felt like they were watching her for something.

"Do you want anything to eat?" Alex asked.

"I'm fine," Lucy said, looking at the food left over on the tray. She puffed out her cheeks and slumped in the seat. "Besides, that all looks kind of gross."

"Lucy," Alex said.

"What? It does," Lucy said.

Lucy slid the paper placemat out from under the food and put it on the table in front of her. Beneath the grease and ketchup stains, Emily could see inked-in activities, things to color and mazes to follow. Lucy traced her finger through the maze, stopping at the dead ends and reversing as she tried to get to the center.

"So, what's the plan?" Lucy asked, pushing the placemat away. She turned to Emily. "Are you coming with us?"

"I don't know," Emily said. "Where are you going?"

"We'll find somewhere. Besides, if you don't come with us, what are you going to do?"

Again, Emily thought of the empty house. "Probably nothing."

"Then let's go." Lucy stood up. She helped her brother out of the booth and leaned against him when they stood together. They both had the same dark hair, large, wide eyes, and pale skin. Lucy's jacket was red and puffy, and she scratched at the place where her fake fur-lined hood itched at her neck. Emily slid out of the booth.

"Do you mind if I stop at the washroom before we go?" Emily asked. She wanted them to have their own time before she joined them. She had a feeling that there were things left unsaid that couldn't be discussed around a stranger.

"Emily," Lucy said, "a) you don't have to ask us. And b) yeah, we'll be out at the van. You know the one." She rolled her eyes in the direction of the parking lot.

It was impossible not to notice the blue van, scuffed, dented, and dirty. Emily dumped the contents of the empty tray into the garbage can.

In the washroom, Emily stared in the mirror. There were dark smudges of mascara under her eyes and her cheeks were flushed from the cold. She brushed her hair with her fingers and ran a wet piece of toilet paper beneath her eyes to remove the specks of mascara that had loosened during her walk in the cold.

In her pocket, her cell phone rang. Emily knew it was her

mom without looking. She clicked the ignore button and the ringing stopped.

Her mom was supposed to be in Victoria for New Year's. She was supposed to have been home at Christmas. Instead she just called and left messages, asking Emily where she was and what she was doing, as if there was nothing wrong. A phone call did not equal the way it felt when someone loved you enough to visit. A phone call didn't equal anything. It didn't take away the fact that her mom had decided to stay in Vancouver to work on writing instead of coming to the island to spend Christmas with her daughter.

Emily washed her hands in the sink. They were cracked from the cold. She carried a small tube of hand lotion in her backpack, something that smelled like vanilla and made her hands feel almost normal again. She left the washroom and went to find Alex and Lucy.

She could see them through the front windshield of the van. Lucy was staring down at the steering wheel instead of at her brother, who had his hand on her shoulder. She glanced up, looking straight at Emily, and immediately folded away the expression that had been there just before. She rolled down the driver's door window.

"Ready to go?" Lucy called.

Emily opened the sliding back door. Jumping back a step, she let out a surprised sound. Inside was a collection of taxidermy animals, their glass eyes dark and shining. That was what creeped her out the most, all those glassy eyes.

Lucy swung around in the driver's seat, smiling wryly.

"Come in and meet the family!"

"What—" Emily struggled.

"Don't worry about them," Lucy said. "Especially Melvin." She pointed out the stuffed dog that was sitting in the back seat closest to the door. "He used to be our cousin Justin's dog. Our dad did that for him. We just haven't dropped him off."

Emily thought that Melvin was the least of her worries.

"You can move them out of the way," Lucy said, "so you can sit down."

Emily didn't want to touch them. Melvin the German Shepherd perched on the seat she was meant to sit on, his face set in a perpetual grin. In the back of the van were the other members of the *family*: stuffed cats and dogs and rabbits, partridge, eagles, and doves. There were larger animals at the rear and Emily did her best to avoid looking in their direction.

She rolled her sleeve down her wrist so she didn't have to touch the dog with her bare hand. Lifting it gently—it was much heavier than she had expected—she moved the stuffed dog onto the next seat. She shut the sliding back door and felt the weight of too many eyes to count. Lucy started the ignition and turned around to smile at her.

"Our dad's a taxidermist."

"He reanimates the dead," Alex added.

"It's one of those jobs that could be either really cool

or really embarrassing when your dad does it," Lucy said. "Turns out it's just really embarrassing. Dad drives me to school in this thing some mornings and he almost always loses an animal. Do you know what it looks like for some dead bird to fall out of the van and onto the sidewalk in front of everyone at your school?"

"Oh, God," Emily said, laughing.

"It sucks," Lucy said. "So most of the time I take the bus."

Melvin looked in Emily's direction with eyes that wouldn't blink. Emily tried to imagine seeing one of these animals fall out of the van in the morning.

"So Em, what do your parents do?" Alex asked.

"Oh," Emily said, so surprised by the question that she didn't even have a chance to remember the vague response she usually had reserved for times like these. "It's just my mom," she said. "She's a journalist. I live with my grandma. My mom's usually traveling."

"What's *that* like?" Lucy asked. "Living with your grandma?"

"Before she went into the hospital, my grandma mostly stayed around the stayed around the house, gardening, reading, cooking. Basically she used to live in the lap of retirement luxury. I'm usually really jealous."

"I want our dad to retire. Instead, he just keeps on doing this stuff and he's getting a pretty serious collection. We're supposed to inherit them," Lucy said.

"The entire taxidermy army," Alex added.

"I'm inheriting a house," Emily said, looking out the side window. "From my grandma."

"With a basement?"

"Yeah, there's a basement."

Lucy looked at her brother with her eyebrows raised.

"Storage space, Alex. For our minions." She jerked her thumb toward the animals. "How'd you know to pick up someone with such value to us?"

"Just got lucky, I guess." Alex winked at Emily.

The van was cold, the cracked metal letting the wind in. It was difficult to hear the radio over the sound of the heat coming out full blast, blurring the sounds in the van into a low hum. A heating vent blew air across the ground at Emily's feet; she could feel it warming her toes through her sneakers. The van bounced against the road, the wheels sticking in every pothole and inching up against the curb. Emily gripped the armrests and watched Lucy's hands on the wheel.

Emily had been the first one in her circle of friends to get her driver's license. Before tonight, she hadn't been in the position to sit in the backseat while someone else her age was driving. And Lucy was someone that she hardly even knew. Not for the first time, Emily tug-of-warred with her choice of going with Lucy and Alex. At least she hadn't agreed to anything. She hadn't agreed to go anywhere in particular. She could get out of the car and go home whenever she wanted to.

Lucy looked at Emily through the rearview mirror. "I still need practice at driving, right?"

"No," Emily said quickly.

Alex turned around again.

"Yes she does. It's even more terrifying from the backseat. The front makes it feel like you can at least lean over and grab the steering wheel if you have to. But I have confidence in you," he told his sister.

"Yeah, yeah, sure you do," she said.

Alex undid his seatbelt and climbed between the front seats to reach the middle of the van. Nimbly, like he was very much experienced in the art of moving taxidermy animals, he lifted Melvin from the seat and set him in the back. In the front, Lucy's cell phone started ringing. She picked it up before it hit the second ring. Seeing her drive one-handed was terrifying.

"There," Alex said. He settled into the seat beside Emily and buckled his seatbelt. "Now we can talk."

"She's cute," Emily said. "Your sister."

"She's also sixteen and definitely not supposed to be driving without our parents," Alex said.

"You can't drive?"

"I'm even worse," he said.

"I don't know if I believe that," Emily said.

Lucy remembered to turn after she'd already passed the corner. Emily's elbow was jarred off the armrest and into the window.

"Lucy," Alex said.

"Hang on, Steph," Lucy said to the person on the other end of the phone. "What?"

"My driving skills. Tell Emily."

Emily wished she wouldn't. Lucy's eyes were already all the way off the road, the fingers of one hand just barely resting on the steering wheel.

"He's terrible. He's so bad he's not even allowed to take the exam. It's why I have to drive the *van*." She pushed the phone back against her ear and resumed talking.

"Why does she have to drive the van?"

Alex looked embarrassed. "Because the car, the new car, crashed. When I was driving."

"Oh," Emily said.

"Is that Stephanie?" Alex asked his sister.

"Yeah. She might be around later tonight."

"Stephanie?" Emily mouthed.

Alex just smiled.

"So why're you inheriting a house?" he asked.

"It's my grandmother's."

"The one in the hospital?"

Emily looked down at her hands.

"They don't think she'll be able to go home again."

"That's hard," he said. "What happened?"

Emily arranged this story in her head, one that would travel through the things that had happened with her and her grandmother.

Back at the hospital after her grandmother's surgery, she couldn't find parking. She circled, the car like a shark, until she did a messy parallel park that seemed too close to the stop sign at the corner of the street. She was sweaty from hurrying when she finally walked through the front doors. It struck her as strange how nothing had changed since she had left a few hours before. There were still people in the cafeteria. The receptionist still sat at her desk with her hand on the computer mouse, navigating files and room numbers and patients on the screen in front of her. Emily stabbed her finger at the up button on the elevator and found her grandmother's room. Her grandmother was back in the hospital bed. There was a white clipboard hanging from the bottom of the bed. It had her grandmother's name —Olive Henderson—written at the top in big block letters, followed by a series of numbers and letters that didn't make any sense to Emily.

Her grandmother was asleep. Her mouth was slightly open; her hands were tucked under the covers. The room was small and white. The window let the sun in. From the fourth floor, Emily could only see the sky and the clouds and the sun. She felt uncomfortable sitting in the room, waiting for her grandmother to wake up. She picked at her cuticles and dug into the skin on her elbows. Everything was fine, she knew that, but there was something about her grandmother in the hospital bed, horizontal and unmoving, that made Emily's heart clench into a tight ball in her chest.

"I thought she'd be getting out of the hospital after a few days. She had to do this physical therapy every day. I hated being home alone and so I did this three-day countdown," Emily said to Alex.

It was strange being in the house alone, even when she thought it was only temporary. It was two stories of cold memory. It was Emily's mom living at home and then getting pregnant and not living at home. It was bedrooms with closed doors, boxes stored and unopened. It was Emily, seventeen, the same age as her mom had been when she left home for Vancouver, pregnant and independent and scared.

Sometimes Emily didn't think her mom could ever have been scared. Even finding out she was going to have a baby —Emily—didn't seem to be enough to throw her off the rails. She went systematically through the steps that she knew would take her from seventeen and pregnant, to a city with a job, to a baby and an apartment, to living alone in Vancouver and leaving Emily, only a year old, with her grandparents on the island.

"So, why *couldn't* your grandmother come home?" Alex asked.

"The woman she did the physical therapy thing with had pneumonia and she passed it to my grandma. It gets easier to catch the older you get. Especially in the hospital."

"Did she know she was going to be in there long term?" Alex asked.

"Not then. Angela, her nurse, said she should just take it one day at a time. But after a week, when nothing had changed, that's when we knew."

Emily remembered the day her grandmother told her that she wouldn't be leaving the hospital. She remembered what came after, when she went home by herself. It was the first night she went home and realized there was a new way of experiencing loneliness. That a house could swallow you up whole.

Emily's hands were clasped tightly together in her lap. It was easy in this car, where she was almost anonymous, unknown, to talk to Alex. She felt like she could tell him the things she had been saving up inside for a long time.

"That doesn't seem fair," he said, "that she could go in healthy and come out with something like that."

"Or not come out," Emily said.

"A lot of stuff with being sick doesn't seem fair. I mean, it seems so arbitrary and random about who gets what and how bad it gets and who gets better and who knows that they just have to realize they're not going to be okay."

"I know," Emily said. She looked out the window and thought about her grandmother left behind at the hospital. She held her hands in her lap and waited for the van to stop.

chapter*eight*

The sliding door of the van creaked open so loudly that Emily thought it would come off in her hands. Lucy stayed in the front seat, reading text messages off the screen of her phone.

"We'll go get some stuff for the night," Alex said.

"For what?" Emily asked, trying to get a sense of what was happening. "Where are we going?"

"We'll find somewhere," Alex said. "You think of anywhere you want to go, let me know. There's nowhere we *need* to go. We'll just make sure we have snacks and things. It's a holiday."

"Okay," Emily said.

The cold felt colder as they exited the warm van. Every breath hung heavy in the air, forming into a small cloud. Emily stuffed her gloved hands into her pockets and walked with Alex to the grocery store. They stood at the front as other customers went around them, nudging past in their own personal hurry. Alex and Emily read the signs that hung above each aisle.

"So you don't have brothers and sisters?" Alex asked.

"No. It's just me."

"Did you ever think you might, though?"

"What do you mean?" Emily asked.

Alex pulled a grin and shrugged his shoulders. "I don't know."

Alex looked like he wanted to say something else, but Emily wasn't sure she wanted to answer questions about her family, or more accurately, her lack of it. Her mom who wasn't there, her dad who she didn't know, who she couldn't know. She used to ask her mom, "Who is he and where is he?" and her mom would go cold and steely and leave the room and then the city and Emily wouldn't see her for weeks at a time.

"Well," Alex said. "Live with Lucy long enough and only-childom starts to seem pretty appealing. There," he said, pointing to the aisle on the end. "Chips and pop are cele-bratory, right?"

"Right," Emily said.

They walked to the last aisle, but all that remained on the shelves were picked-over bags of chips and boxes of crackers.

"What's your favorite kind of chips?" Alex asked.

"You mean between bacon and cracked black pepper?"

"Mmm," Alex said, wincing.

"Oh, wait!" Emily said.

She moved a few bags to reveal a perfect row of barbeque chips. Alex picked up one of the bags and wrinkled it until it made a crinkling sound.

"You speak their language."

"Take me to your leader," Emily said in a mechanical voice.

"Does not compute. Does not compute," Alex responded, removing another bag from the shelf.

When Alex bent forward to catch a slipping bag of potato chips, Emily saw a small bit of blood spreading just above his upper lip.

"Alex. Your nose," she said. "I think it's bleeding."

Alex raised his finger to his face and watched it come away red.

"Shit." He reached into his back pocket and pulled out a piece of Kleenex. It was wrinkled and bunched, the two sheets coming apart at the edges. He held it to his nose.

"It's hot in here," Emily said. "With the heat and our coats on and everything."

"Yeah. That's probably it."

Emily took the two bags of potato chips from him.

"I'll go pay for these. You go back to the car and fix that."

"Thanks, Em." Alex pulled an old brown wallet from his back jeans pocket and tossed it to Emily. "I'll see you in a second?"

They went off in different directions, Alex toward the front doors and Emily to the rows of pop bottles at the back of the store. She grabbed two and held them tight between her arm and her side. She carried the potato chips in her other hand and brought everything to the cashier.

Even in the express line the conveyor belt moved slowly, the debit machines timed-out, and, because everyone was in a hurry, no one was going to make it out quickly. When Emily was finally able to deposit the food at the till, she still had to wait for the woman ahead of her to go through. The cashier was flipping through the produce codes to find the right one.

"I know it's here," she said.

Her forehead was shiny with sweat and her ponytail was falling out of its elastic.

"Take your time," the woman ahead of Emily said, but with a tone that said, *Hurry up*, instead.

Emily opened Alex's wallet to pull out a twenty-dollar bill. Behind her she could hear the shifting of feet, bags crackling, and cans clacking together as tired people re-arranged the things in their baskets, trying to forget about the wait.

There wasn't a driver's license in Alex's wallet, or a pass-port, but stuffed into a pocket was his student ID card from Churchill High School. Curious, Emily nudged it halfway out of the pocket.

His picture had been bent in half until a crease formed across the lower half of his face. The plastic lamination was coming apart at the corners. Alex was smiling hugely, and he looked neatly put together. The Alex she had met tonight and the Alex in the picture were almost two different people.

Emily had lived in the same house in the same city and gone to the same school in the same neighborhood all her life. She knew the things that happened to the people she knew to make them stop looking like they always had. She knew when their parents got divorced or when their siblings left for college or when their grandparents died. She wondered what had happened to Alex to turn him from the person in the picture to the person that she knew, skinny and tired and frayed.

"Next."

Emily shoved the card back into the wallet. She handed over a twenty-dollar bill and collected the change and the two plastic bags.

chapter*nine*

Alex could see his sister sitting inside the van, tapping her foot on the floor. She had her elbow resting on the plastic ledge of the window. When she saw her brother coming out of the grocery store, she unlocked the doors and stepped outside.

"Hey," Alex said to Lucy as he walked to the van, Kleenex still pressed to his nose, "no problems?"

"No problems," Lucy answered. "How are you doing? It's been a while since you've been out, you know."

"I'm okay. I mean, I guess I'm a little slow. I couldn't keep up to Emily when we were walking over here. And then this happened," he said, pointing to his bloody nose.

Lucy pulled out a couple of tissues from the Kleenex box in the back of the car.

"I want to take you back," she said.

"We talked about this. If I have to go, I'll tell you. This is okay."

"I know," Lucy said. "Okay. I'm good. You're okay?" Alex figured she was trying to reassure herself, asking it like a question for him to answer again.

"I'm okay."

"She's pretty," Lucy said, looking toward the grocery store. She talked as she examined Alex, checking his nose, looking at the Kleenex, trying to find another packet of clean tissue. She spoke as if to reassure him, to make him forget for a few minutes the things that were happening to him.

"Yeah. She's really nice, too," Alex said.

Lucy monitored the progress of the nosebleed. Alex hoped this one would stop more quickly than some he'd had lately.

"I can't believe you're here," Lucy said. "I'm so used to seeing you as an inside person. You know like how there's inside cats and inside dogs that stick to the rooms of a house? And then there's outdoor cats and outdoor dogs that roam around and have adventures and hunt at nighttime?"

"Thanks, Lucy," Alex said, "for comparing me to an inside dog."

But when Alex thought about it, it was mostly true. For the last few months, he couldn't get out of bed until after lunch. It wasn't that he would be sleeping. He would be lying in his bed with his eyes squeezed shut trying not to throw up, and if he had to, concentrating even harder to make sure it was into the bucket on the floor. He was the same level of tired whether he stayed up all night or if he slept half the day. Alex always felt like his arms weren't heavy but the bones inside were. He could picture them, as if he were looking at a dancing skeleton taped to the door at Halloween, with limbs made out of paper rotating on thumbtack joints. The hospital had made things worse. Two weeks without leaving his single narrow room.

It had been three years since he was diagnosed with leukemia for the first time. Rounds of chemo and radiation had eventually put it into remission, but over the summer, it came back. He could feel it digging its heels in *everywhere*, knobby joints and bony ridges that stuck in tight to his skin. It had felt different the second time. And when Dr. Davies had walked into Alex's room with his hands together and said, "acute lymphoblastic leukemia" and "survival rates" and "MRI" and "blood count," all Alex heard was: "Alex Hobbs, you're screwed."

He had stopped the chemo treatments in October. He had hair again but only because there wasn't any reason to continue treatments. To *waste* treatments, Alex thought.

Alex's mom cried at everything. It made him want to leave the room and get the hell out of there, but, in the saddest way, it made him want to cry, too. Because if she couldn't stop crying, it meant that *there was no hope*. Every single thing that could happen to him in a month or a year or *ten* years wouldn't.

Through the front windows of the grocery store, Alex watched Emily standing in line, balancing bags of chips and bottles of pop in her arms. He grinned at Lucy, who had been watching him the entire time, concern written all over her face.

"Alex, your nosebleed hasn't stopped yet, has it?" Lucy asked.

Alex twitched his nose in the bundle of Kleenex. He felt a fresh flow of blood start up again.

"No," he said. "It's still going."

"Squeeze harder," she said, and she hung onto the bridge of his nose and pressed tight.

"Lucy," Alex said.

"I know. Act normal," she said. "We're all acting normal."

Only a few months ago, Alex had been sitting in the guidance counselor's office at school, talking about getting ready for his senior year.

"You're going to need to do some resumé packing, Alex," Mr. Jordan said. He reclined in his chair and looked so relaxed that Alex wouldn't have been surprised if he had swung his feet onto the top of the desk and clomped them down in the middle of his crumpled papers and spilled pens.

"I think I'm doing Leadership next year," Alex said.

"That's a good start. You should try Student Council. I bet they could use you there."

"I guess."

Mr. Jordan leaned forward across his desk, picked up a pen, and started tapping it against the side of his computer. There was already a skinny crack running along the edge of the screen.

"I checked out your transcript. It's good. You put any thought into what you might want to take at college?" It wasn't really a question. He just wanted Alex to talk.

Alex *had* thought about it. At night, when there wasn't anyone around. When he wasn't completely sure about something, the worst thing he could do was to talk to someone about it. If he said he might be interested in journalism, the next thing he'd know, his parents would be telling him about their editor friend at some local newspaper and he'd be signed up for a summer internship. But by then, Alex would already be thinking about something else. There wasn't anything really permanent about what he was thinking about. They were quick, those thoughts. They were just ideas.

Alex didn't say much more to Mr. Jordan. He was given a list of a few more volunteer opportunities and sent out into the hall. There was a row of chairs filled with students at the door. Stephanie was sitting in the last chair and when Alex saw her, he forgot just about everything he had talked to Mr. Jordan about.

Stephanie moved over until there was enough room for the two of them to share the chair.

"Mr. Jordan tell you your future?" she asked, like he was a

fortune teller sitting in a dim room with a crystal ball.

"Better," Alex said, handing her the paper Mr. Jordan had given him. "He mapped out my entire next year."

Stephanie looked at it, squinting. Alex knew she needed glasses for reading things up close, but she never wore them. The bridge of her nose wrinkled when she narrowed her eyes and it always made Alex's stomach flip.

"What? You're going to do extracurricular activities?" she asked, separating the words into their syllables.

"Maybe," Alex said.

"Student Council? Yearbook? Model UN?"

The door to Mr. Jordan's office opened and the next person in line moved down. Alex stood up and Stephanie moved into the next seat.

"I better go back to class," he said.

"I'll see you after school."

Alex used to drive Stephanie home most days. But that was before school stopped being an option for him. Normal school, normal girlfriend, normal everything.

Six months later and it was almost like it hadn't even happened.

Now he was confined to the hospital, trying to remember what it meant to walk down a hallway with people pressing in from the side. He used to be able to figure things out. Now it took other people to get him unstuck, unglued from where he got when he was alone. Lucy had to peel him back like Velcro from a place that was like pre-death and post-life.

Alex let go of Lucy's hand, and leaned forward in his seat.

"You remember the last time we did something like this?" Alex asked her.

"We've never done anything like this."

"Come on," Alex said. "I mean the last time me and you went somewhere together."

Lucy thought about it. She tipped her head to the side. "The museum," she said.

"I liked that," Alex said.

Lucy had surprised him, telling him to get his jacket and put his shoes on. He hadn't known right away where they were going.

"I wrote this cool essay for Mr. Brummell the other day," Lucy had said as they waited at the bus stop. "On *Lord of the Rings*. He wrote on the board, 'The theme is betrayal,' since we were doing *Julius Caesar*, and I'm like, 'That's a pretty common theme across a lot of books,' and Mr. Brummell said, 'Is it? Tell me more.' So I started going on about Boromir and how he totally betrays Frodo when he tries to take the ring and Mr. Brummell was like, 'Hey, write an essay about that,' and I said, 'Really?' and he said, 'Sure. Just make sure it connects to Shakespeare at the end.'"

"Mr. Brummell's a good guy." Alex knew it had been a while since his sister had done any homework. Sometimes he felt like doing it for her. He missed going to school so much that he figured he'd use her homework to make him feel like he was normal. But his mom caught him doing it once and she gave him an hour-long talk about what would happen to Lucy if he did all of her work for her. Alex still did her math sometimes. Lucy hated math.

"He'd be a better guy if he waived all of the assignments for this semester. He's still making me do all the old ones."

"Yeah, well, I guess that's what you'd expect."

They walked around downtown. Alex stood in front of the windows to a pizza place. He was looking at his reflection. His hair had grown back in a little. He looked almost like he had before.

"Look," Lucy said, pointing down the street. "There's the bookstore where you bought *Lord of the Rings* for me."

"Changed your life," Alex said.

"It did."

They crossed at the lights and Alex squeezed Lucy's arm when they were standing in front of the museum.

"Hey, we haven't been here in years."

They went through the front doors and bought two tickets at the counter. Then they went around the corner to the narrow escalator.

"Let's see the animals first," Lucy said.

Their dad did the taxidermy upkeep for the animal displays. He'd be at the museum a few times a year, picking up damaged displays and taking them back to his shop to work on.

Alex and Lucy stood in front of a scene with some deer. There were four of them, standing by a painted scene of woods and flowers. Alex leaned into his sister. That 3D into 2D thing on the dioramas always got Alex. The place where the 3D animal displays ended and the background painting on the wall behind started up in 2D always made him stop and take another look. He would think it was real, and then he would look up and see that painted wall and know that it wasn't.

In the van, waiting for Emily to come back, Alex wondered if it would be the last time he and Lucy did something normal like visiting a museum. He wondered if this would be the last time it would be so easy.

Alex patted his hands on his thighs and looked out the window. He saw Emily leaving the store. He put his hand on Lucy's shoulder.

"That was a really good day," he said.

"I know," she said. "I know."

"There," Alex said, pointing out Emily to Lucy. "She's coming back."

*chapter**ten***

The back doors of the van were open. Alex pressed a bundle of Kleenex to his nostrils while Lucy held the bridge of his nose very tightly between her thumb and forefinger.

"Through your mouth, Alex. You know that."

"I doe dat but I can't breeve. Your fingers are in da way."

"You're lucky you've got a veteran here."

As Emily walked toward them, Lucy said, "You got everything!"

Alex pulled the Kleenex away from his nose and Emily handed him his wallet.

"Is it any better?" she asked.

"Should be," Alex said, smiling at her. "Long as I don't bleed out."

"But it hasn't stopped yet," Emily said. "Nosebleeds don't usually last that long."

"I'm fine," Alex said, giving her a reassuring smile.

He stood up but stumbled, falling sideways into Emily. She put her hand on his elbow. Their heels were touching, leaning into one another as she tried to keep him standing.

"Maybe you should sit, Alex," Lucy said quietly.

"Nah. We should get going."

Emily watched the exchange, a bystander to the easy way they were as siblings. Lucy held onto Alex's elbow, where the cuff of his jacket had rolled up.

"You're freezing," Lucy said, rubbing her hand up and down his arm.

"It's cold," he said and then he smiled.

"I'll turn on the heat."

Lucy crawled into the driver's seat from the passenger's side, her heel kicking at the glove compartment.

"Come on, Em," Alex said, climbing into the back.

The bags of chips crunched between the seats. In the front, Lucy stuck the key in the ignition and turned. The van made a scratchy, robotic sound, the engine snorting and shuddering, and then it became very still.

Without the heat, the inside of the van was as cold as the outside.

"It's dead?" Lucy asked.

Alex switched seats with Lucy, planting himself behind the steering wheel. All he could do was pump the gas a few times while turning the key in the ignition. But it didn't matter how many times he tried, the van didn't start again.

"It's dead," he confirmed.

Emily hadn't done up her seatbelt yet. She leaned forward in between them. "We could just take the bus," she said.

"Where?" Lucy asked.

For the first time that night, Emily realized that she could steer the night in a particular direction.

"We could go to my house. We can pick up my grandma's car and drive that instead."

"Yeah, that sounds good," Lucy said. "When's the next bus coming?"

Lucy grabbed one of the bags of chips from the back and opened it. A burst of salty air puffed out of the aluminum bag and filled the car with a greasy smell. Emily checked the bus schedule on her phone. She didn't take this route home very often.

"The next bus isn't coming for an hour," Emily said.

"An hour? Why so long?"

"It's New Year's, Lucy," Alex said, raising his eyebrows at her. "It's a holiday. We're kind of lucky there's a bus coming at all."

"Can we try starting this thing again?" Lucy asked.

She and Alex each took another try at turning the key in the ignition, hoping one of them had the technique that would start the vehicle and take them out of the strip mall. Then Emily stepped on the gas pedal a couple of times while she joggled the key. The metal grating sound that followed made her pull the key out fast and toss it to Alex. He didn't have any more success than Emily did. His wrist twisted with the effort of turning the key.

"You're like Elastic Man," Lucy said, pointing at his arm. His skin looked fake and rubber, forming unnatural folds with the exaggerated twist of his wrist.

Lucy tried again. She brought her feet down on the gas and brake pedals and pulled at the clutch in a last-ditch attempt to make the car move. Then she pocketed the keys, got out of the car, and stood in front of Alex and Emily with her hands on her hips.

"What are we going to do for an hour?"

"Sit at the bus stop?" Alex said.

Emily rubbed at her arms. "You don't think it's too cold out? We're all kind of pale and cold-looking already."

Lucy looked at her brother and then at Emily. He shrugged at her, but Lucy's hands dropped from her hips and hung at her sides, palms up.

"Yeah, maybe we should figure out something else," Lucy said.

"I'm fine to sit at the bus stop," Alex said.

"Not for an hour."

The strip mall across from the restaurant was long and low. None of the buildings were more than one story high. There were a couple of fast-food places, the signs colorful and recognizable, with cars lining up in the drive-thrus.

Emily had become good at getting meals from outside

the house, buying a sandwich at the cafeteria on her way home or pulling up to a drive-thru by the hospital. She lied to her grandmother every day about what she was eating and how often she was using the kitchen. "I went grocery shopping on the weekend so I made spaghetti," she would say, or "There were some eggs so I made an omelet and toast." The truth was, Emily hadn't used the kitchen since her grandmother went to the hospital. Her mom had taken the ferry over from Vancouver and stayed for three days right after her grandmother had received the diagnosis of pneumonia, and Emily had met her at the terminal and driven her down to Victoria. But her mom didn't cook either. She ordered pizza and spread the box flap open over the dining room table or she took Emily out for Chinese food and sushi downtown.

"Em, are you going to eat that?" she asked at a place on the wharf, her chopsticks agile and quick.

"No."

Her mom plucked a sushi roll off Emily's plate and popped the entire thing in her mouth.

"I'm going to stay for two more days, honey, but then I have to get back to the mainland. I just need you to tell me that you're going to be okay with all of this. I spoke for a long time with her doctor today, and your grandmother's going to have to stay at the hospital. This is one of the last things that I'd wish to happen, Em, but I just need to know that you can handle yourself. You'll keep going to school every day?

I'll call and check in on you, but I need to get back to work."

"I'll be fine," Emily said, monotone and dead.

"Good," her mom said, visibly relieved. "We still have a few days together. How about I take you shopping tomorrow? We'll come back downtown and hit the boutiques. You like doing that, don't you?"

"I have school tomorrow."

"Then we'll go after."

"I've been visiting Grandma after school."

"Oh, Em, I'll spend the whole day there. You don't even have to worry about it. I think it's a good idea that we spend some time together tomorrow. Let's do that, okay?"

Two days later, her mom left and Emily started her new routine. It mostly involved avoiding the house as much as possible, visiting her grandmother after school, and screening her mom's phone calls.

Emily took another look around the strip mall. She was trying to process everything she had told Alex and Lucy. Usually, she spent almost all her energy trying not to think about what was happening in her own life. But tonight she had let everything out.

"We could go bowling until the bus comes," Emily said, surprising herself.

"Where?" Lucy said.

"There's an alley in this strip mall. It's on the other side of the grocery store," Emily said. She knew because she passed it on the days that she came here from the hospital.

"You know what?" Alex said. "That sounds okay."

"You can't bowl," Lucy said.

"Why not?"

Lucy looked at him pointedly, as if it was obvious, but Emily couldn't see why.

She rubbed her hands on her legs. They were cold and stiff under her jeans. She led Lucy and Alex around the front of the grocery store to the other side of the strip mall. The lights were on outside the building and there was a low glow coming from behind the windows. The lights that surrounded the illuminated bowling pins chased each other around and around, the tail never catching up to the front of the pattern. The cement walls were chipped and the cracked cement was filled with uneven lines of tar. The lights buzzed and hummed, even crackled with the energy of keeping the lights lit.

"Em, is this place, you know, condemned?" Lucy asked.

"It's fine," Emily said, but she didn't know what it looked like inside. "I mean, this isn't bad, right?"

Lucy leaned her shoulder on the glass door. It pushed open. They had been sitting in the dark parking lot long enough that the dim interior of the bowling alley seemed as natural as anything. She thought about how hard it would be to come in here in the middle of the day. The dark inside would make it hard to see coming in right out of the sun on a hot day.

"Actually, it's not that bad," Lucy said.

There was an arcade to the right, blinking with lights. The bowling lanes were on the left. Straight ahead was a counter that stretched halfway down the bowling alley. There were shoes to rent and a place to get pizza. Emily could feel the steady rumble from the bowling lanes through the floor.

"We haven't done this since some birthday party, I think," Alex said.

"*My* birthday party," Lucy said. "Mom did a bowling party for me until I was ten or something," she explained to Emily. "Alex always came, too, even though he's older and also a boy."

"Your friends like me," Alex said.

"Some of them."

Lucy leaned in and whispered to Emily, "He used to date my best friend."

"Oh."

Emily looked between them. She tried to imagine that triangle of brother, sister, best friend. She couldn't see a reason that Alex wouldn't have a girlfriend. He looked like the guys she knew, familiar and recognizable. There was an unmistakable sense that he was in high school, and she thought he was probably really popular there. Usually her guard went up the second she knew someone she liked had a girlfriend. She felt self-conscious and had a desire to form an immediate ranking between her and a girl that she didn't even know. Alex was different. She couldn't imagine being together with Alex like that, in the way she could imagine herself with other people her age. She wanted *this*—the comfort and ease that came from not having expectations for something more.

She thought back to that picture in his wallet. She wondered when that had happened, the changeover from being one way to another, and if the change in him had anything to do with why Alex wasn't dating Lucy's best friend anymore.

Finally Lucy sighed and went toward the back of the bowling alley. She walked up and rested her elbows on the counter. The man behind the counter took their shoe sizes.

"I'm a seven, he's an eleven, and Em?" She looked at Emily. "What are you, Em?"

"Eight."

"And she's an eight," Lucy said.

They were given the lane at the very end of the bowling alley, the one that hugged up against the white wall. It was covered in framed pictures of celebrities, musicians, and athletes, some of them signed and some of them just taken out of magazines and given a sturdy backing. Emily kicked off her boots and put on her pair of bowling shoes. They smelled musty and chemical. Lucy had a tough time getting her boots off her feet. She was wearing two pairs of thick socks that padded the bottom of her boots. She took one layer off, balled them up, and stuffed them in her jacket pocket.

"Do you want me to get those?" Emily asked Alex. He was bent over his shoelaces, undoing them one-handed. His other hand was reaching for the bowling shoes on the floor by their lane. He was trying to do both at once, but Emily could tell it wasn't easy.

"I've got it," he said.

Sometimes Emily wondered if he was okay. He did things in an exaggerated way, his legs moving too fast before then falling into small, short, staccato steps. His hands would snap open and closed in rapid succession, his fingers moving nervously until he covered them with the too-long sleeves of his jacket.

"You have to put our names in the computer," Lucy said to Emily. "Can you do it? I'm going to get something to drink."

"Sure," Emily said.

She sat in the chair in front of the computer and started typing in their names. Alex looked up at the screen that dropped from the roof to hang above their lane, his eyebrows almost to the top of his forehead.

"What kind of names are you giving us?" Alex asked her.

"What do you mean?" Emily had already typed in their names. She had Lucy going first, then Alex, and her at the end. She looked down the bowling lane. The gutters were deep and empty. Emily already figured that was where her ball was going to end up, even if she tried hard to hit the bowling pins.

"I mean, don't you usually do funny names and stuff? Like, nicknames?"

"Do you have a nickname?"

"No," Alex said.

"Does Lucy?"

"If she does, she didn't tell me. But you do. Kind of," Alex said.

"Me?"

"Yeah, you get to be Em, right?"

Emily's name had never been shortened by anyone. She didn't get the "sweetie, honey, baby" from her mom. She wasn't called Em by her friends. She had never been pulled out of the formal three-syllable label. Like an Elizabeth who was never a Liz, or a Katherine who was never a Kat. Emily leaned over the computer and replaced her name with "Em." She sat back in her seat. She was losing the tightness in her chest, the stress in her shoulders.

"Lucy's really struggling with bringing us a pitcher of pop," Alex said. "Look at her coming over."

Lucy was balancing a too-full pitcher of pop in one hand and three glasses in the other. She'd bought a pizza. The box was hanging over the edges of her right forearm, teetering dangerously from side to side like a seesaw. She set the drinks and pizza on the table beside them. She opened the pizza box and lifted a long strand of cheese from the cardboard.

"Thanks for the help," Lucy said. "Am I up first?"

"Yeah," Alex said. "Surprise surprise."

"Emily, this was a really good idea," Lucy said. She turned the ends of Emily's hair until it twisted into a bun. "Your hair looks really nice up," Lucy said. "Doesn't it Alex?"

Alex looked back at Emily and Lucy. He had been looking at the monitor above the lane. "Yeah, you look really nice," he said.

Emily moved her hands to hold her hair up at the back of her neck. Her mom had sent a voucher for Emily to get a free haircut downtown. She hadn't gone to use it yet and she really wasn't sure if she was going to.

"Okay, okay, I'm going," Lucy said. "You guys are next so you better watch." She selected a bowling ball, a solid pink one. There were some with swirling colors, but this one was Pepto-Bismol pink all the way through. Lucy hesitated, looking like she was testing it out first.

"Lucy, come on already," Alex said.

Lucy was standing at the top of the lane, peering down at the bowling pins and trying to figure out angles.

She threw the bowling ball. The pink streak of color slid down the lane, wavering back and forth across the shiny boards. Lucy's right foot had slid out in front of her and it lay across the line that separated the normal floor from the lane. They watched the bowling ball roll into the gutter with a solid thud.

"I take it back," Lucy said. "I want to do something else. Let's go back to the grocery store or something."

Alex held a piece of pizza by the crust and his bowling ball in the other. He took a bite and went up to the start of the lane. The ball went into the gutter and Alex sat back down in the chair.

"That wore you out?" Emily asked, picking up a bowling ball, a turquoise one with yellow swirls of color. Alex breathed in shakily and, even though Emily thought she had made a joke, he really wasn't looking great.

"Losing does that, you know," Alex said.

Emily stepped up to the line. She hadn't bowled for a long time. It seemed like something that was relegated to elementary school parties. The carbonation from the pop sat uncomfortably in her chest. She was self-conscious standing at the line with Alex and Lucy behind her, watching. In the other lanes, the pins went down. The rumbling sound of the weighted bowling ball sliding down the waxed boards covered the music playing from the speakers.

"We'll still love you if you suck," Lucy said.

"We'll probably love you more," Alex said.

Emily held the bowling ball. It was an easy thing, she knew, for some people to say that they loved you. She'd had friends who would say it like it was nothing. But in her family, an "I love you" was a pulled tooth, given up with difficulty. She didn't end her phone calls with her mom with anything more serious than a "goodbye." Even when she helped her grandmother up to bed in the house every night because of her hip, she only said to Emily,

"Thank you. Good night. See you in the morning."

Emily threw the bowling ball down the lane. It went into the gutter almost immediately. She felt a hand on her shoulder.

"Guess we all suck," Lucy said. "You want some pizza?"

Even though she'd just eaten with Alex at the restaurant, Emily grabbed a slice of pizza and ate the entire thing, crust to end. Emily took a couple of Lucy's turns and one for Alex. None of them did very well.

"How much more time do we have to kill?" Lucy asked, after throwing the pink bowling ball down the lane.

"Fifteen minutes?" Emily said.

"Maybe we should just head over to the bus stop," Alex said. He picked up their empty cups and the pizza box and took them to the counter.

Lucy shared one of the chairs with Emily. Their sides were pressed together and their elbows almost interlocked. Lucy had discarded the bowling shoes and had her boots on again. Emily had helped her pull them back on over the thick double pair of woolen socks.

"It's stupid because it's not even cold," Lucy said, holding the boot by the heel and trying to pull it up.

"It's a little bit cold," Emily said. "It's winter."

"It's the west coast," Lucy said.

"So, that just means we don't know any better."

"Emily, you're pretty cool," Lucy said. "I'm glad you came with us tonight."

"Yeah, well, I can't believe I did it," she said, then saw Lucy's face fall. "Not because of you and Alex. It's just, I've really got this routine. It's kind of a wake-up-go-to-school-go-to-the-hospital-go-home-sleep thing. It's the only way I've been able to keep this up for the last month."

She looked across the bowling alley. She thought the person coming toward them was Alex, back from getting rid of the garbage. She lifted her hand in a wave.

"Emily, I thought it was you! Like, I wasn't sure from far away so I said I'd come over and check." Before, Emily would have said Veronica was her best friend, but she wasn't really sure what she'd call her now, as she leaned against the table.

"Hi," Emily said, uneasily. "How's it going?"

"We're just on the other side. We've been here for an hour or something and we're sticking around before we go to a couple of parties. Josh and Kevin are here. You want to come say hi?"

Lucy was giving Emily a look. "Lucy," Emily said, "this is Veronica. Veronica, this is Lucy."

"Oh, hey, your friend can come, too, if she wants. We're just bowling. Do you even have plans tonight? It seems like I haven't seen you in forever."

Veronica was tall, taller than Emily, with her brown hair pulled back into a high ponytail. She was wearing tights with a skirt and a long-sleeved shirt tucked into the waistband. She had on tall brown boots that ended just below her knees. Remembering everything that had happened between them, Emily felt like she was falling apart.

"We're leaving soon," Emily said.

"Soon isn't now. Just come over and say hi."

Alex came back right then. His presence made a box out of the four of them, standing by the computer.

"This is Alex," Emily explained. "Lucy's his sister."

"I guess I'll leave you to it," Veronica said. "You'll call me before school starts again?"

"Sure," Emily said, even though she knew she wouldn't. "I'll give you a call."

"Because it feels like I haven't seen you in forever."

"I know."

Veronica leaned over and hugged Emily tight, and then she walked away.

"Who was that?" Lucy asked. "I mean, *Veronica*, but, who is she?"

"She's my best friend," Emily said. "She was my best friend. She probably still is."

"You want to make that a little bit more complicated?" Alex asked.

"It's fine," Emily said. "We just haven't talked a lot since my grandma went into the hospital. I guess I haven't been around as much."

That was the easy way to put it. That was the half-lie and the leaving-things-out.

It fell apart with Veronica a week after Emily found out her grandmother wasn't leaving the hospital. That week was in-between time. It was Emily trying to figure out her new routine, one that involved an empty house and a hospital and school that still kept on going.

"We'll figure this out," Veronica said, after Emily told her. "You can come stay at my house whenever you want."

"Thanks," Emily said. "I'm going to try to stay home right now. I don't want to leave it empty. I don't think my grandma wants the house left empty."

"She wouldn't have to know. It'd be less lonely."

"I'll think about it," Emily said.

Veronica offered to come over every day after school, but Emily had to go to the hospital first. She had to sit with her grandmother until visiting hours were over. At first she wasn't sure how long she'd be able to keep going. She hated seeing her grandmother in that bed, skinny and fragile and declining. But by the end of the week, she yearned for it; she wanted that place to go to because the hospital was another building that wasn't her home. She started staying longer and longer. She sat in the wooden chair beside her grandmother's bed until the nurses would come and remind her it was time for her to leave, and that she could return the next day.

Veronica would call when Emily got home from the hospital and ask if she could come over, and Emily always made up an excuse. She was too tired, or she had to call her mom,

or she had to pack up some things to take to the hospital the
next day.

"Stop avoiding me," Veronica said, one night on the
phone.

"I'm not. I'm just busy," Emily said.

"No, you're not. You're just sitting in your house alone."

"I'm not."

"Things are going to change," Veronica said. "She'll come
home."

"She's not going to come home."

"I know your grandma. She's not going to stay in there
forever."

"You think she has a choice?"

Emily had hung up the phone. She locked the doors. She
turned off the TV. She went upstairs and climbed into bed
and didn't get out until the morning.

"She was concerned," Alex said, as she told them. "That's
all."

"I know," Emily said. "Still."

Emily didn't know if it was just that it had been so long
since she'd had someone to talk to like this, but something
made it easy to sit with Alex and Lucy and tell them the
things that she had told no one else. Between Emily and her
grandmother and Emily and her mom was something vast
and uncrossed. Emily knew that. They didn't share things
like normal people did. They didn't provide the scaffolding
that told the reasons why things were the way they were.

The Friday night after Veronica had called, Emily came home from the hospital. She was tired. The end of the week was the worst. She hated the way everything drained out of her. Emily got off the bus a couple of blocks away from her house, took her keys out of her pocket, and unlocked the door.

The dark house was instantly illuminated, before she'd even had a chance to turn on the lights. The living room was full of people from school. They came out from behind furniture and from the kitchen, holding red plastic cups with drinks in them, some of them sloshing up and over the top and onto the carpet. Veronica stood in the middle of it all, yelling, "Surprise!" She leapt forward to hug Emily. Someone turned on the music. There was a loud thumping that crept into Emily's head, prodding at her brain like a pair of fingers.

"What are you doing?" Emily asked.

"You need a break. You're so stressed. I thought I'd throw you a party," Veronica said.

"How'd you get in the house?"

Veronica rolled her eyes, reached into her pocket, and pulled out a single key. "You showed me where the spare is, remember?" She leaned in and whispered to Emily, "Under the flower pot in the backyard. I've known since elementary school."

"You remembered."

"God, of course I did," Veronica said. "Come on. Let me

get you something to drink."

"No," Emily said. "No. I don't want this."

Veronica was pulling Emily's arm. When Emily didn't move, the smile on Veronica's face constricted.

"Don't be weird, Em. You need this."

"These are my grandma's things," Emily said. Already a lamp had fallen off a side table. Someone had moved a row of pictures from the mantelpiece so they could lift themselves up there and sit down. "She wouldn't want anyone in the house."

"We'll clean up after. Just have fun first."

"No." Emily shrugged off Veronica's hand where it still held onto her arm. "Get everyone out of here."

Veronica pulled at the bottom of her skirt. She inched her sleeves down over her wrists.

"It's not the end of the world. Your grandma in the hospital? You know it's not forever. I don't know why you're so upset about this. It's not like you."

"You don't know what it's like."

"Because you haven't told me."

"I'm telling you now. I don't want this. I want everyone out." Emily went to the stairs.

Veronica stayed in the middle of the living room, watching her go. Her eyebrows went together, wrinkling at the bridge of her nose. "You don't have to do this," she said.

Emily ignored her. She went upstairs, shut the door to her bedroom, and locked it, listening to the solid click of the doorknob. Emily went to her bed and sat down. She smoothed out the sheets with the palms of her hands. She took off her boots and kicked them into the closet. By the time she was done, the music had stopped. It turned off in the middle of a song, ending as abruptly as it had begun. She tried not to listen to the voices of people she knew, complaining about having to leave. Finally, she heard the front door close. She had thought everyone had gone when there was a knock at her door.

"Emily? It's Veronica."

Emily stayed quiet. She took off her socks and tossed them at the laundry basket. They hit the edge and fell on the carpet.

"Can I come in?"

Emily pulled back her sheets. She climbed into bed. The soft mattress felt so much better than the hard-backed chair in the hospital room. It melted into her spine and kneaded out the way it felt to sit next to her grandma and know she was dying.

Eventually, Veronica went back downstairs. The front door opened and closed. Emily heard the lock slide into place.

After that, Veronica didn't call. Emily didn't miss her. She was sucked into her routine. School, hospital, home. School, hospital, home. Home played the smallest role; the most insignificant amount of time was spent there. The new way she did things became her understanding of normal.

Emily, Alex, and Lucy took their bowling shoes back to the counter and stopped to look in the arcade for a few minutes. They had to walk by the lane where Veronica was bowling on their way out. Emily walked out of the building with her head down.

"I still think bowling was a really good idea, even if you had to run into her," Lucy said.

"Yeah, it was a lot of fun," Emily said. "And that's fine. It really is."

"So, bus stop," Alex said. "Which way?"

"What about the van?" Emily asked, as they passed by it in the parking lot. "Do we need to do something about it?"

"We'll pick it up tomorrow," Lucy said.

They didn't seem as concerned about it as she was. She didn't think she'd be able to leave her grandmother's car in a strip mall parking lot overnight on New Year's. She didn't think she'd be as calm and "Pick it up in the morning" cool about it as Lucy.

"So, I guess we're going to my house?" Emily said.

Alex and Lucy grabbed her arms, one on each side.

"You're really awesome for doing this," Lucy said.

"It's fun," Emily said.

As they crossed the street to the bus stop, she took one more look behind her: at the van full of taxidermy animals, at the bowling alley, at the grocery store. She had been to more places in one night than she had been in the last month. Seeing Veronica at the bowling alley had brought that back to her—a reminder of how things had been and how they had changed. She wondered what would happen if she left Alex and Lucy and went back to the bowling alley. It might not be so hard to go back to how things used to be with Veronica. Maybe.

She let Alex and Lucy drag her forward across the parking lot, their arms linked and looped together. They crossed the street, Emily buoyed up and warm, between the two siblings.

chapter*eleven*

Lucy had been watching Alex, side eye, the entire time he bowled. It hadn't been her idea for this to happen. She had wanted to find Emily as much as Alex had, but Alex's reason was furious and urgent, while Lucy wanted to wait and feel it out before jumping in and meeting her. She had gone along with Alex because that was what she did now. If he suggested something that had behind it a desire or a need, Lucy said yes and made it happen. Still, she didn't like the way the night was already draining him. His face was pale and drawn. Watching him deteriorate in the time between the grocery store and the bowling alley pulled hard at Lucy's chest.

It seemed so obvious now, the way he had changed since he had gone back to the hospital. He'd lost weight. His hair had been balding from chemo and then shaved in defiance and then it had grown back in again. But he was still here, standing at the bus stop, looking at Lucy and Emily and giving them one of his Alex smiles. He was so much there, standing in front of them, that Lucy wondered how she was supposed to believe he was just going to disappear.

Still, she had her cell phone in her pocket, ready if she needed to call someone.

Stephanie had been texting her all night. She didn't know about the plan. She didn't know about Emily. But Stephanie was her best friend, so Lucy kept texting back, trying to put off the question, "What are you doing for New Year's?" as long as she could. She couldn't lose Stephanie as her friend. Lately, she was one of the only reasons Lucy was still able to go to school every day.

Without Alex, Lucy's school routine was long and uncomfortable. It started when she pushed on the metal side door that opened up right next to her locker. Her locker was in the options wing, where all of the classrooms for food and sewing and cosmetology and band were squeezed down one narrow hallway. It was loud and busy and there were smells spilling into the hallway from the rooms. Lucy would take most of her books out of her backpack and throw them into her locker. She would hang onto her books for Math and English and get out of that hallway before the bell rang.

She'd encounter the first hurdle almost the second after she slammed her locker and walked to class.

"Lucy, how's your brother?" It would be Mrs. Murphy, Alex's old Biology teacher. She was taller than Lucy and she had curly hair that she tied back with a colored bandana.

"He's fine," she'd say. "He's at home."

"I just finished a book I thought he might like. If you stop by my classroom after school, I can give it to you to take to him."

"Yeah, sure."

"Say hi to Alex for me," Mr. Stavely said later. He had taught Alex Social Studies the year before.

"Will do."

"Hey Lucy."

She would almost say, "Yeah, yeah, he's doing fine, I'll pick up your book, I'll pass it on, he says hi back," when she'd realize it was Stephanie. She'd slouch her shoulders, relieved at not having to try very hard anymore.

The difference between the teachers who would ask about Alex and Stephanie was that the teachers only had that one-sentence question. They only knew him from one place, in that school, and everything they had to talk about or ask about fit in a tiny handful of words.

Stephanie was a little bit taller than Lucy. She had long blonde hair and she wore T-shirts that belonged to her dad before he left Stephanie and her mom. The shirts had fading patterns and logos that were hard to see because they had gone through the wash and probably through alcohol and maybe even vomit to get distressed just like that. Lucy knew that lots of people liked Stephanie, but she still got shy and disinterested around other people. She was Lucy's best friend. Alex liked her so much that he asked her out and they became something like boyfriend and girlfriend or together or whatever.

English class always went by the fastest. Sometimes Mr. Brummell, her English teacher, turned on the radio and let them listen to music while they analyzed the important plot points of a short story.

There was this thing that Lucy liked the best about her English teacher. He had a *Lord of the Rings* poster in his classroom that reinforced to Lucy that he was different from her other teachers. It was a poster of Gandalf in the Mines of Moria. There was a speech bubble where he says, "You shall not pass!" Lucy knew Gandalf was saying the words to a demon that was standing in his way. She knew that the demon couldn't pass because of those words. Instead, he just falls over the edge of the cliff. Mr. Brummell's poster had Gandalf standing in those mines but the speech bubble was expanded to, "If you don't study, you shall not pass!" Lucy thought it was almost like he had a real sense of humor.

The only problem with Mr. Brummell was that he was always getting on Lucy's case about her homework.

"Lucy, I'll need you to hand in your essay by tomorrow. I think that's the extension we agreed on," Mr. Brummell said.

"Yeah, yeah," she said, still writing. She was working on a journal entry about *1984*. She didn't really get why they were reading the book in class. It seemed like it was written a hundred years ago. Still, Mr. Brummell didn't mind when she was cool with him. There was no pressure. "I'll get it in."

"Glad to hear it."

But every time he asked, Lucy heard a small voice in the back of her head remind her, "Mr. Brummell isn't getting the essay by the weekend." Lucy hadn't done homework for weeks. Mr. Brummell understood what was happening to Alex.

She used to leave school with Stephanie in the afternoon, but always after English class. It was the only one she didn't want to miss. There was a time when she was leaving school like that every day. Now she stayed at school a lot more. There were fewer visits to the beach and to movies and almost no visits to Stephanie's house for lunch and hanging around in the backyard. Because the school was on an automated messaging system, Lucy had to be careful about how much she missed. The prerecorded voice would phone the house whenever she did, to let her parents know immediately. She imagined sometimes that it said something like, "Mr. and Mrs. Hobbs, your daughter Lucy was not in school today and, moreover, she has not been in school at all this week, and I think you will find that we have a very strict attendance policy, and, if she misses much more, we will not be able to pass her into grade twelve next year."

She had missed a lot of school at the beginning, when Alex's leukemia came back. The answering machine at home had been disconnected, so there had been no more of those messages home. Because Alex had been placed on a list, and his contact information sold to drug and pharmaceutical companies, they would get home, press play, and hear, "You have one hundred and twelve new messages." In order to delete them, someone would have to listen to them first. There wasn't a "delete all" option. Lucy's dad had pulled it out of the wall one night after dinner.

No one wanted to hear messages about drugs that were supposed to help with particular symptoms, especially when they were listed. "If your son is experiencing nausea, loss of appetite, weight loss, dizziness, weakness ..." and they would all be sitting in the living room thinking, "Yep, that about sums it up."

It wasn't until there was a letter in the mail about Lucy's attendance that her mom went to buy a new answering machine. Her parents weren't going to let her absences get that out of control again. Now, most of the time, she stayed at school all day.

Stephanie helped a lot. Lucy didn't think she could do it without her.

But Stephanie wasn't the only one she was getting texts from tonight. There were a dozen from her mom.

The hospital called, Alex is missing.

Lucy, have you heard from Alex?

Where is your brother?

Lucy, come home, we need to find him.

There were messages from her dad.

Don't do anything. Stay where you are and I'll come and pick you up.

If Emily is with you and Alex, go back to the hospital. We can figure this out.

Get your brother to the hospital.

So he thought Emily might be there, too. Her mom didn't know about that. Lucy wondered when she would find out.

Lucy tucked her phone back into her pocket. She wiped her hands, clammy with nervousness, on her jeans. She took her gloves out of her pocket and waited for the bus.

chapter*twelve*

Emily watched Lucy read the text messages off her cell phone. It took almost an entire minute for her to scroll through them all. Alex didn't seem to notice. He retied his shoe and fixed his jacket. Lucy's face stayed controlled and level. She didn't give any hint of what the messages said.

"I hate the bus," Lucy said, when she was done. She slumped against the plastic wall of the bus shelter. Alex and Emily were inside, sitting on the long wooden bench. There were strange stains, wads of gum, and crumbled cigarette butts on the bench itself, and they had carefully found the cleanest part to sit on.

"Taking the bus isn't that bad," Emily said.

"It is when you've been used to driving," Lucy said.

"You're not even supposed to be driving," Alex said.

"And just how exactly would you be here if I hadn't?"

"Well, we'll have a car soon, anyway," Emily said.

There was one in the garage, her grandmother's, not driven since she had taken it to the hospital one month before. When Emily went to visit, she always took the bus. It was too difficult to deal with hospital parking, easier just to be dropped off nearby and find her way in. But she could drive if she wanted to. All she needed were the keys.

And then there was the other side of going home. Emily could stay there. Running into Veronica had thrown her off the evening. Part of her was considering getting home, offering to drive Alex and Lucy to their house, and then going to bed. There wasn't any reason to keep going.

"Thanks," Alex said, nudging her knee with his. "Hey Lucy? Nice of Em to do this, right?"

"Yeah, it really is," Lucy said. She leaned farther still into the plastic wall, her jacket pressing up like a 2D impression.

Soon the bus pulled up against the curb of the sidewalk, the brakes making a screeching sound that made Emily's teeth hurt. The doors creaked open and warmth seeped out of the bus onto the cold street. They filed in one by one and swiped their bus passes.

The bus wasn't full, but the way the few people who were on it stared at them made it feel as if they were standing in front of an audience. They found three seats together near the back. Alex and Emily sat side by side and Lucy squeezed in across from them. All of their knees were touching. Emily tried to hold hers still.

"So," Alex said. "You do this every day?"

"Not this route," Emily said, leaning her head back, "but yeah, every day."

"That sucks," Lucy said.

"Sometimes."

"I bet it gives you time to think," Alex said.

"Time to read, mostly," Emily said. She patted her backpack where it sat between her feet. Every time I visit my grandma I get papers and pamphlets. Information, mostly."

"Oh, we've got a lot of those," Lucy said.

"What for? Your friend?" Emily asked.

"Yeah," Alex said.

"Let's see what you've got," Lucy said, holding out her hand.

Emily unzipped her backpack and pulled out a stack of papers, their edges creased and rumpled. Lucy pressed them into the top of her thigh, smoothing them out carefully.

The fact that someone else was doing the work of reading the papers made Emily feel like a layer of uncertainty was coming unfolded from her chest. She crossed her arms in front of her until her elbow was inching into Alex's, and watched the lampposts outside blur by.

"What does your Grandma think about all this?" Alex asked.

Lucy flipped through the papers, skimming the information Emily had read over and over.

"I haven't really talked to her about it," she said, turning a handful of pages so that they fluttered.

"I guess she probably knows everything, from the doctor," Alex said.

But Emily's grandmother would not talk about her pneumonia. To her, it didn't exist except for when it manifested in fits of coughing that forced her to use the oxygen mask that hung beside the bed.

"Before the papers and pamphlets, I used to spend hours on the computer, looking up information about the disease that I could talk to my grandma about," Emily said. It had made the first few nights at home alone bearable. It felt like she had a purpose for being there. She could figure it out. "But when I went to my grandma with all this information about strengthening her immune system or foods that she could eat that might help with her breathing, she wouldn't listen."

"Would things like that help?" Alex asked. "I mean, the non-medication side."

"They might," Emily said. "But she didn't want to try."

When Emily brought food, drinks, or nutritional supplements that she'd read about, her grandmother would leave them untouched. Eventually she gave up. She stopped bringing the things that her grandmother didn't want, the things that acted as an acknowledgement of her disease.

Talking to her mom on the telephone was different. Her chest would grow so tight with the knowledge that there was nothing she could do to help her grandmother. But her mom was already resigned to that fact. "Visit her as often as you can," she'd say. "That's all you can do, Emily. That's it." Her mom wasn't visiting. Emily didn't know what to do with advice that was given without being followed by the person who was giving it.

"Sometimes you can get a nurse or a doctor to go over all of that," Alex said. "It might be better coming from one of them."

"I really tried. There's not enough time. And my grandma doesn't think anything's going to work. She really doesn't."

Emily had figured out what she needed to know, but listening to the information circle around her as Lucy and Alex asked questions and read the papers, broke something down in her. The loneliness started chipping apart.

There were twenty stops between the hospital and Emily's house. She looked out the window when she thought they were close and waited until she recognized something familiar.

"Here," she said. The bus stop was close to where Emily lived. They got off the bus and walked around the corner. It was three blocks to Emily's house.

The house Emily lived in with her grandmother was a tall, narrow two-story. There was a garden in the back and a gate in the front. The lights were all turned off inside. Emily usually tried to remember to leave the porch light on when she left the house, so she wouldn't have to come home alone to a dark house, but she hadn't done that today. She wondered where Alex and Lucy lived. She wondered how close they were in the city. She thought their house would have the lights on.

Emily turned her key in the lock of the front door and pushed. She fumbled along the inside wall for the switch. Watery light flooded across the floor. It shone on the windows and reflected back the image of the three of them standing in the hall. The clock above the couch said nine o'clock.

"Okay," Emily said. "The car's in the garage."

Lucy walked into the living room and collapsed on the couch. She sighed and closed her eyes. "Ugh, my legs."

"It was a ten-minute walk, Lucy," Alex said, but Emily thought that he sounded tired, too.

"But I don't walk anywhere."

"Well, I mean, we can stay for a while if you want," Emily said.

"Yes," Lucy said. "We want."

"Bathroom?" Alex asked.

"There's one upstairs."

He nodded and headed toward the stairs. Emily sat down on the couch beside Lucy.

"He's probably going up there to make sure he looks okay," Lucy said.

"He looks fine," Emily said.

"You think?" Lucy asked.

Emily remembered the picture from Alex's wallet. Maybe he didn't look okay. She wanted to ask Lucy if there was a reason why, but she couldn't tell her that she'd opened his wallet and looked all the way through.

Lucy ran her fingers through her hair. She held the ends between her fingers and let them fall in front of her face. She tucked her hair behind her ears again and moved the pillow pressing into her side.

"Can I have a glass of water?" Lucy asked, jumping off the couch.

"Yeah. The glasses are in the kitchen." Emily stood up and led the way to the back of the house. She turned on the light. There was an old Brita water filter on the top shelf. Emily filled it periodically, whenever she remembered that it was there. She poured a glass for herself and one for Lucy.

Emily perched on the counter. It was clean and spotless, untouched since her grandmother went into the hospital. The fridge was mostly empty.

"So it's really just you since your grandma went into the hospital?" Lucy asked.

"It's really just me."

"Why do you go to school?"

Emily laughed. "Because I have to."

"I'd just stay at home all day. I mean, that's what Alex does. Sometimes I'll stay home with him and stuff, but most of the time my mom sends me to school. 'Lucy Hobbs, get your ass on the bus or I'm driving you there myself.'" She made her voice rise one octave higher to imitate her mom.

"Alex doesn't go to school?"

"Well, I mean, he does," Lucy said, picking at her cuticle. "He does. Sometimes he just stays home when he's sick and stuff. But I mean, what about your mom? Where's she?"

"Um, she calls," Emily said. "She stayed the weekend we found out my grandma couldn't leave the hospital. But she really has her own life. It sounds weird when I explain it to other people, but it's not."

"I don't get it," Lucy said. "She doesn't live here?"

"No," Emily said. "She lives in Vancouver. She's a writer. I mean, freelance. She works for newspapers and magazines and she goes back and forth across the country sometimes. Not all the time. Most of the time she lives in her apartment in the city."

"How did that happen?"

"She had me when she was seventeen. My grandma kicked her out of the house."

"And after that, your mom left you here?"

Emily nodded. She swung her feet against the counter. Her heels hit against the drawers. "When I was still a baby. She brought me back and left me with my grandparents. I guess I get it. She wasn't ready. I'm the same age she was when she had me. I don't know what I'd do if the same thing happened. "Catching the expression on Lucy's face, she said, "It's really okay. It's just the way it is. I've always liked living with my grandma."

"I guess. But even when you were older? You didn't want to move and live with her?"

"I had friends and school and this house. I didn't want to move. My mom didn't push it enough for me to think I should go with her."

"What about your dad?" Lucy asked.

Emily's heels were tap dancing. Her left heel hit the cupboard hard enough that it bounced open and hit her in the calf. She kept her legs still and held her hands on her knees. The last time someone had asked her about her dad was in elementary school. It was Veronica, when she came over to Emily's house for the first time.

"How come your parents are so old?" she asked, after Emily's grandmother left them in Emily's bedroom with a plate of cookies. Her grandfather had been in the front yard when Emily and Veronica had walked home from school.

"They're not my parents. They're my grandparents."

It had always bothered Veronica that Emily didn't know who her father was. Veronica pressed her about it a couple of times throughout junior high and high school, but Emily wouldn't let it grow into a conversation. She had learned when she was young that her mom would not answer the question: "Who is my dad?"

She was in elementary school the first time she asked, on the phone from her grandparents' house in Victoria. Her mom went quiet on the other end of the line and eventually made an excuse and hung up. Emily didn't talk to her mom for three weeks after that, even though she tried to call the apartment in Vancouver.

She tried the question out again when she was in middle school, and once when she started high school. Her mom's reaction was the same. She fell off the face of the planet.

"I have no idea who my dad is," Emily said.

"Huh," Lucy said.

Emily squeezed her knees together and took a drink from her glass of water.

"Have you ever tried looking for him?" Lucy asked, her voice trailing up with a lilt at the end.

"I don't even know where to start."

"The Internet," Lucy said. "Or, like, a yearbook or something. Doesn't your mom have any of those?"

"There were boxes in the basement and stuff, but my mom cleared them out a couple of years ago. There's not really anything left of hers here anymore. My grandma thinks my mom snoops when she's here. She hates how much she looks around the house."

"Still, that doesn't mean you can't look for your dad."

"My mom wouldn't talk to me," Emily said. "It's this thing, this really big thing. It's been seventeen years. If I started now, it just seems like I'd lose my mom over it."

"It doesn't seem like she's even around, though," Lucy said.

"I guess having my mom, even if she's far away and she

doesn't come back often, it's still better than not having anyone."

Lucy swirled the water around inside her glass. She opened and closed the fridge. "There's nothing in here," she said.

"I usually eat at the hospital," Emily said.

"That stuff sucks," Lucy said. "I mean, it's pretty shitty. It's hospital food."

"The cafeteria isn't bad. It's mostly from businesses downtown."

"Hey, Em," Lucy said. "I'm really sorry your mom won't let you know your dad."

"I don't know. I mean, what if he's an asshole? What if he wants nothing to do with me, and my mom knows that, and that's why I've never met him?"

Lucy shrugged. "Or he could be really nice. He could have a family."

"That'd be even worse. Wouldn't it?"

"I don't know," Lucy said. "Siblings are nice. I mean, look at me and Alex."

"It doesn't seem like there's that many like you two" Emily kicked at the cupboards. She wrapped her hair around her wrist and then unraveled it again. "I don't know. I really don't. There are some times that I want to know more than anything. But then I think about my mom and I don't know if I can do it."

Emily didn't want to talk about it anymore. She got down

off the counter. "I think I'm going to get changed. Are you okay down here?"

"I'm fine," Lucy said. "You look really nice already, though."

"I'm just going to look," Emily said. "I'll be right back."

Emily didn't go upstairs. She could hear Alex up there, the sink tap in the bathroom running on high. She went into the guest bedroom downstairs where her mom stayed when she came to visit. For maybe two years, Emily would tape a "Welcome Home" poster to the outside of the door. She'd write the letters in alternating colors—a red W, yellow E, orange L, and on and on, her twenty-four pack of pencil crayons rolling open on the table. She never repeated a color, even if she had to use black and brown and the color of yellow that she didn't like. There was nothing else to indicate that the only person who used this room was Emily's mom. The sheets and duvet were her grandmother's. They weren't embellished or decorated. They were plain white. There was a blanket folded on the end of the bed with tassels on all four sides. In the winter, that blanket was usually folded over the back of one of the chairs in the living room. Emily would pull it down and wrap herself up with it. When she had long hair, almost all the way down her back, it would get wrapped up in those knitted tassels and knot them all together, tying the strings in unmanageable knots. She'd find her grandmother sitting with the blanket at the kitchen table, a pair of scissors in her hand, cutting out the hair and freeing the tassels. After watching her do that half a dozen times, Emily stopped using the blanket. They left it folded in the guest bedroom for whenever Emily's mom came to visit, with her short-kept haircut that stopped at her shoulders.

The room didn't have a closet, but a giant wardrobe pushed into the corner between the wall and the window had heavy wooden doors carved with swirling, looping lines. Emily shut the door to the guest bedroom and opened the wardrobe. A handful of folded sweaters on the first shelf were her grandfather's. He had passed away a year and a half before. He had a stroke when he was moving boxes in the basement. Emily had been at school when it happened.

After her grandfather passed away, her grandmother got rid of most of his things. She boxed them up and took them to the Salvation Army. Emily's mom had fought with her about that, her voice loud on the other end of the phone. "I don't care if it's hard having his things around. I don't care. I told you I'd be coming back again this weekend. I told you there were things of his that I wanted. Don't tell me they're all gone. Don't tell me that."

"Kate, I couldn't have them around here. You're not here until Saturday. It had to be done."

"Stop saying that. You could have waited for one more week. You could have waited."

Her mom didn't come that weekend. Emily helped her grandmother box up a few things of her grandfather's that had been left over: his reading glasses, his winter jacket, a pair of running shoes. They went to the post office together and sent the package to her mom's apartment in Vancouver.

Emily was prepared for her grandmother's eventual passing away. She had known for a while now. She didn't know which was better: the knowing and preparation or the not knowing and suddenness. She thought there must be a third option, something easier.

Emily ran her hands through the sweaters in the wardrobe. For some reason, her grandmother had held back these few. She wondered if her mom noticed them here, in this wardrobe, when she came to Victoria to visit.

There were two extra pillows on the top shelf of the wardrobe. There was a folded plaid blanket for the winter. It would get cold in the house starting in November. Sometimes the heat would blow through the vents intermittently, but it depended on her grandmother and the heating bill and things that Emily wondered if she even knew about.

On a long metal bar between the shelves of the wardrobe were several hangers that held a few things her mom had left behind. Emily didn't know if it was deliberate—if these things were here so she didn't have to pack as much when she visited, or if they were left accidentally when her mom returned to Vancouver, left behind and forgotten. It made sense for some of them to be left behind. A pair of baggy jeans. A khaki jacket. A printed T-shirt that was used for pajamas. But there were things that Emily wanted to believe had been left on purpose. There were three skirts, patterned and printed, that her mom wore all the time. There was a dress, grey and woolen, that hung long enough to touch the next shelf down. She couldn't believe in her mom coming home to stay—there was nothing that made her believe in that—but there was permanence to the wardrobe.

Emily put on the grey dress. She couldn't remember having seen her mom wear it before. She thought it had been in the wardrobe for a long time. She found a pair of black tights in the sock drawer, the balled-up socks looped together into small woolen balls. She shut the wardrobe and looked at herself in the full-length mirror that leaned against the wall. She smoothed out the dress, hips to knees.

"Huh," she said, looking in the mirror. Usually when she was out all day, she came home with dark circles under her eyes and a general feeling of being creased and wrinkled. She had just been out the entire day and part of the evening, but she looked like she had just woken up from a long nap.

Emily could still hear the sound of water, but she didn't know if it was coming from Alex in the bathroom upstairs or from Lucy in the kitchen down the hall. It was strange to hear the sounds of other people in the house. She was so used to identifying her sounds as the only sounds. The pop of the TV when she turned it off at the end of the night. The click of the lock on the front door that she checked and double-checked and triple-checked. The creak of the fridge opening and closing on the odd occasion she ate here. She was the epicenter of the house. Everything went on around her. Now she was triangulated with Alex and Lucy. The house felt fuller now than it ever had. Even when it had been Emily, her grandparents, and her mom all in the house at the same time, there was a disconnection between all of them that made them into isolated dots scattered across a floor plan of the house. This—her and Lucy and Alex—had some kind of pattern to it.

Emily opened a few more drawers before she left the bedroom. Nothing had changed since her mom had visited back when they first had news of the pneumonia. She had come for a few days, nothing more, and left again. She didn't travel and stay overnight anymore. Anything in the wardrobe was from pre-sickness, left in the house when they learned that the hospital would grow to be like an extra appendage.

Now Emily's mom would occasionally take the seaplane from Vancouver in the morning and spend the day at the hospital. She would leave before Emily got out of school. Emily would find her grandmother alone in the room, sitting up in bed and eager to tell her about the visit.

"Don't take that personally," her grandmother told her, over and over. "You know how she is. You know how she feels protective of her time."

"If you know when she's coming, can't you tell me? I can miss school for a day."

"She doesn't call beforehand. And I don't want you missing school. This is such an important year for you, Emily."

"Still, it's just one day. Call me next time she's here."

"We'll see."

Emily couldn't count the number of times she'd scoured this room after her mom had left, looking for clues that would explain her mom's silence on so many things. But her mom kept her secrets tidy and organized.

Emily slipped on her boots and went back to the kitchen wondering at the way her house could suddenly be full with strangers, people she hadn't met until tonight. She could push the rest aside for now. She had time. Time for Emily was endless.

chapter*thirteen*

Lucy stayed in the kitchen when Emily left. Curious, she opened the cupboards and the fridge, looking at what Emily kept here. There was half a jug of milk in the fridge and a couple of boxes of cereal. Lucy couldn't find much else, except for bulk cans and baking supplies that sat unused and aging. The garbage can was full of takeout packages and plastic utensils.

It had been Alex's idea for Lucy to drive the van and his idea to leave the hospital. Neither of them had planned exactly what would happen next. They were waiting for the right moment, the time that both of them thought was right to tell her. Lucy was still unsure about the "telling her" thing. That had been Alex's idea, too. "Lucy, we have to find her and tell her. We have to meet her. We have to spend time with her."

"Okay, okay," Lucy said, going along because Alex didn't have a ton of decisions that he could make. "But she won't even know us. Why do you think she'll come?"

"That's the thing. We have to make her like us."

"How do we do that?"

It hadn't been that much work at all. And now, Lucy thought, it was almost time. Emily's hesitance showed on her face, a reluctance to keep going with them even though they were having fun. And Lucy wanted more than anything to get her brother back to the hospital. He was looking worse and worse as the night went on.

Lucy was trying to keep a close watch on him, but while he was upstairs, she had a chance to look around. The kitchen was so different than the one at their house. Here, it was all clean counters and no clutter and empty cupboards. Lucy's mom and dad kept the kitchen pantry full. There were half-full mugs and cups left out on the counter until someone remembered to put them in the sink. The light above the oven was always left on. Lucy and Alex would meet in the kitchen in the middle of the night and sit at the kitchen table with a bowl of refrigerated leftovers between them. They would go through pizza, lasagna, pasta salad, and stew. The small overhead light would keep it cozy and covert.

From looking around Emily's kitchen, Lucy knew that nothing like that happened here. Maybe it never had. Lucy thought Emily had completely accepted her grandmother

being in the hospital. The evidence was everywhere. She
had settled into her new way of living, and now she was just
going through the motions.

Alex's leukemia was something that Lucy had become
used to. It was funny how they had all accepted it into
their lives, this resignation that Alex had something that
would be with him until the end, and the realization that
he would not leave the hospital again. It became a place
of permanence. They had all crowded into the skinny,
white room on Christmas morning, with all of the presents and wrapping paper covering the floor. That was the
morning Lucy had the secret in her head, the "I know
who she is." She hadn't told Alex then. She had waited.

Alex's leukemia was once a terrifying thing. It still was;
Lucy had just learned how to keep her fear and worry from
rising past this invisible line in her chest, this place she had
marked below her heart. When she started to feel for Alex,
her heart would squeeze and hurt and she'd know she had
let the line rise too high.

Lucy heard a sound from down the hall, the direction
Emily had gone. She stood still in the kitchen, and then
slid onto the countertop. She rested the back of her head
against the closed cupboard doors.

When his leukemia came back, Alex and Lucy were both
in high school. She had gotten used to seeing him in the
cafeteria; she was aware of the routine of avoiding some of
his friends, these older guys who would tease her and yell

at her in the hall when her brother wasn't around. The last time Lucy had seen Alex at school was the day his cancer came back. He had collapsed in class. An ambulance had to come and take him to the hospital.

No one told her that the reason the ambulance had come to the school was to take her brother away. She just sat in class a few floors up and watched it all happen out the window until someone remembered to tell her, "Oh, by the way, Lucy, that was your brother that the ambulance came for," and she had to go and collect the books from his desk and take the bus out of there.

Lucy straightened the dishcloths that hung from the oven door. They were checkered red and white. They had similar ones in their kitchen, except they were always sopping with water from when Alex used them to dry dishes. That was his thing in the kitchen. Lucy was supposed to put them away in the cupboards, after Alex dried them. They had a dishwasher but it hadn't worked for a year. Lucy knew it would only take a phone call to fix it, but a phone call seemed like too much sometimes, with everything that was happening with Alex.

Lucy guessed a lot had happened in this kitchen. A few weeks before, they had what Lucy's dad called "an Event" in their kitchen at home.

Lucy had been sick in class and Stephanie had driven her home. Alex opened the door to both of them. Lucy knew she looked terrible. She had run to the washroom at school and seen her face in the mirror. It was pasty white and her eyes had been squeezed shut.

"What happened?" Alex asked.

"I think it's the flu. She um...threw up," Stephanie said.

"In *Math*."

"I don't blame you," Alex said.

"Mr. Lyell sent her home," Stephanie said.

Stephanie and Alex went to the kitchen while Lucy lay on the couch, pulling her knees up tight to her chest. Throwing up made her think about Alex. He had dealt with this almost every day when he was going through chemotherapy. He would lie face down on the couch groaning and trying to keep his nausea under control.

Lucy sat up carefully on the couch. She wrapped her hands around her legs. Her head felt cloudy and unstable, as if any movement to one side or the other would throw her entire body off balance. She could hear Alex and Stephanie in the kitchen. If there was one good thing to come out of throwing up in class, it was getting Alex and Stephanie back into the same room again. Lucy didn't know how long it had been since they had seen each other. Alex's leukemia had become an invisible wall that formed around him. People left. People didn't know how to deal with the way he was now. Stephanie did, but Alex had learned how to be okay with loneliness. He wasn't watching doors close against the people he knew; he was closing them.

Lucy steadied herself and walked down the hall. Some-times she felt like she could be the link that was sometimes needed between Alex and Stephanie. She had been the one thing they had in common. She wanted to keep them together. Lucy stood by the kitchen, the wall concealing the fact that she was eavesdropping.

"It was pretty bad," Stephanie said to Alex, pulling open the fridge door. "Mr. Lyell was writing something on the board and Lucy just leaned out into the aisle and threw up all over the floor."

"We'll never convince her to go back to school."

"What about you? Are you coming back?"

"No," Alex said. "I'm at the hospital at least twice a week and in between ..."

"Yeah," Stephanie said. "I thought so."

It wasn't awkward, but it wasn't how it had been before. Lucy knew it was close to being over, but neither Alex nor Stephanie was going to be the one to end it. They weren't pretending but pretty close to it. Stephanie was still Stephanie and Alex was still Alex but there was something stuck in between. It was like a great big piece of metal had depolarized them.

Stephanie set the glass of ginger ale on the counter and it made a clinking sound. Lucy peered around the kitchen door, staying close to the wall so they couldn't see her. Stephanie's hands were hanging at her sides. But then she raised one and put it on Alex's cheek.

"I don't know what to do," she said. And then she kissed him. Lucy stared at the carpet and considered going back down the hallway.

"Alex, what are you doing?" their mom asked, her voice unnaturally high, as she and their dad walked in through the back door.

Alex and Stephanie pulled away so fast. Stephanie's hand slid from Alex's cheek and knocked the glass of ginger ale off the counter. The glass broke on the floor and a puddle of liquid seeped into the toes of Alex's socks.

"I'd better go," Stephanie said, the glass crunching under her shoes.

Her cheeks were flushed and the back of her neck was red as she hurried out of the kitchen. Lucy would call her later.

Alex and Lucy's parents were quiet, standing around the broken glass, even after the front door had opened and closed and it was just family in the house again.

"You *know*," their mom said. She was still dressed in a skirt and blouse from work. Their dad was standing behind her, looking between his wife and his son. "You *know* you're supposed to stay away from anyone who might have something. A cold, the flu, you know what could happen."

"Stephanie's not sick, Mom."

"But your sister is. Stephanie could have whatever that is. Your immune system ..."

Lucy felt her stomach drop. She hadn't even thought

about the fact that she could pass this to Alex. She had just been thinking about getting home, and then there was also the thing about getting Stephanie and Alex together. Being sick hadn't even factored into it.

"I wasn't supposed to let Lucy into the house?"

"That's not what your mother's saying, Alex," their dad said, the first time he'd spoken.

"It's exactly what I'm saying," their mom said.

"Come on, honey," their dad said. He put his hand on her elbow but she pulled it away.

"Don't. This is serious. It's Alex's *health*."

"Yeah. It's mine," Alex said. "So let me figure it out."

Alex's socks were thick and he walked across the glass. It crunched under his feet but it didn't get through.

Just for tonight, Lucy had to pretend Alex wasn't going to die. She used to pretend a lot, when Alex was sitting at home for the months he couldn't go to school, that he had been suspended or that it was just summer vacation, and she'd miss school, too, to stay at home with him and make the lie more palpable. When he was in the hospital, she pretended he had gone to get surgery and he was in recovery. Now, while they drove from place to place in Victoria, Lucy pretended more than she ever had that they were having a normal New Year's Eve. It was almost believable. Alex was out and walking around. He was doing things he hadn't done for so long. It was easy to close her eyes and imagine this was the way it was going to be.

But underneath that was the invisible line that inched toward her heart. It was climbing higher and higher as the night went on. Finding Emily had been time sensitive. If they had waited any longer, Alex wouldn't get to know her. The entire evening was a reminder of the way things really were. Time was trickling down. They would need to tell her soon.

chapter*fourteen*

Alex lay on the bed upstairs. Emily's room was almost the same size as the one he had at home, only hers had one long wall that slanted toward the arch of the ceiling. Her bed was in between two windows that looked out into the backyard. Alex had pulled the blinds and tried to look down at the grass below, but his reflection bounced off the window like a mirror. He sat down on the bed. Even in that blurry glass, he could see the circles under his eyes and the tiredness in his face.

Alex looked at Emily's dresser. Two of the drawers were open, articles of clothing left unfolded and hanging over the sides. The top of the dresser was covered in loose items: makeup, a hairbrush, a hairdryer, a bundle of necklaces, their chains linked together, three candles, and a jar filled with buttons. There was a bookshelf in the corner, books with their spines turned out and neatly organized. Alex smiled, thinking about the difference between Emily's bookshelf and his sister's. Lucy's shelves at home were packed with *Lord of the Rings* books. Emily had a variety. There were classics new young adult books, and *Harry Potter*. Next to those, pictures hugged the edges of the shelves, all of them with Emily and one other person.

There was one picture of Emily with a woman with short brown hair and eyes that crinkled at the corners when she smiled. Now, Alex knew she was Emily's mom. Because of everything he had found out, he knew what Emily's family looked like. The photograph was taken of just their faces. Alex picked it up, put it down, and picked it up again. He didn't think they looked alike. He thought they looked so different.

Emily's room was a lot like Lucy's, Alex thought. It was cluttered, but clean. It was lived in, but it wasn't worn out and tired. Alex's was a mess. He used to spend so much time in it that he became used to the beat-up look of clothes on the floor, overflowing garbage, and dirty plates. When the phone calls had started coming, the strange ones that had led him to tonight, Alex always managed to find it before it stopped ringing.

The first phone call came at the beginning of December, before he went back to the hospital for good.

"Hello?"

There was silence on the other end of the line and it lasted so long that he almost hung up.

"Hello," said a woman's voice. It was soft and quiet and seemed stuck inside the phone, unable to make its way out through the other end. She left a long pause that was filled by a static buzz. "I'm sorry. I wasn't expecting anyone to pick up."

"Yeah, well," Alex said.

"Is Chris there?" she asked. Chris was his dad.

"No."

She didn't say anything else for a very long time.

"Okay. Thank you," she said.

The calls came like that every day. Alex would pick up the phone, listen to the voice, and tell the woman that his dad wasn't at home. Then she'd hang up and they'd go through it all again the next day. Alex tried to find out why she was calling. He'd ask why she needed to talk to his dad; he'd offer to take a message; he told her when his dad was home. Still, she never called in the evening. To Alex, it was like she would only call in a particular window of time. She wouldn't venture into the dinner hour. Alex thought about those phone calls a lot, but he didn't tell his dad about them. He didn't want the woman to find him.

Now he was at Emily's house, and those phone calls were irrevocably linked to everything he was throwing himself into. He knew it was worth it. He knew there wasn't anything he'd rather spend this one night doing. Still, he was getting tired. He laid his head back on the pillow and closed his eyes.

chapter*fifteen*

E mily went upstairs.

The bathroom was empty on the top floor. Alex hadn't come back downstairs, and she wondered where he was. Her feet quiet on the carpet, she walked down the hallway until she came to her grandmother's room. Although the door was propped halfway open, inside it was dark and empty.

She found Alex in the last room at the end of the hall, her room, sprawled out on the bed with the small bedside lamp on. She hoped she hadn't left anything embarrassing out that he might see.

She let her knuckle fall against the doorframe until he looked up.

"Hey," he said.

His head was resting on the pillow and he was staring

up at the ceiling. Emily walked to the edge of the bed and sat down, narrowly avoiding tripping on her way there. At the end of her bed was a large chest that her grandmother called "Emily's Treasure Chest," and the corner always caught the side of her foot. It was filled with things from when she was younger, stuffed toys and diaries and pictures torn from magazines.

"I didn't mean to stay up here for so long," Alex said. "You know how you see a bed and just instantly think about sleep and get tired?"

"I know," she said. "It's still a while until midnight."

"That's why I'm resting."

"Lucy's in the kitchen."

"Yeah, you don't want to lose track of her," Alex said, smiling, but in that same moment his face changed completely, wrinkling into a grimace.

"Are you okay?" Emily asked.

"Yeah," Alex said, but his forehead remained deeply furrowed. "I think it's the cold. It was cold out, right?"

"Really cold," Emily agreed.

"I just have to warm up."

His face stayed creased by something she couldn't see.

"Don't," Emily said, taking her fingers and smoothing out the lines in his forehead. "You look like you're auditioning for *Star Trek*."

"You watch *Star Trek*?"

"I'm a sucker for daytime television," Emily said.

"Me too," Alex said. "Like, I can't get enough of talk shows. And *American Gladiators*," he added, his eyes still closed.

"Jerry Springer?"

"You bet."

"Maury?"

"With all the paternity testing?"

"Soaps?"

"Em, that's a secret I'm taking to my grave."

It was hard to imagine Alex as a soap opera watcher. Small admissions were slowly being drawn out of each of them.

"Which ones do you like?"

"I'm not telling you."

"*Days of Our Lives*? *General Hospital*? *All My Children*?"

"Nope," Alex said, shaking his head from side to side.

"Oh, Alex. You don't watch that one." She could see his smile growing wider and she could feel her own in response as she guessed.

"Em ..."

"It's *Passions*, isn't it? You watch *Passions*."

Alex laughed, this deep sound from the back of his throat.

"That's pathetic, you know," Emily continued, enjoying hearing him laugh. "There is a *witch* in that show."

"Whatever," he said. The wrinkles on his forehead were gone and he looked like he was back to normal. "Look, it's been a long year, okay?"

"Yeah. For me, too," she said, thinking about her grandmother.

Emily turned toward the sound of Lucy's footsteps on the stairs.

"What are you guys *doing*?" Lucy asked, leaning against the doorframe.

Alex swung his legs to the side of the bed.

"Talking."

"Yeah, well, talk about what you want to do," Lucy said. "Where are we going to go?"

"We can stay here if you want." But as soon as she said it, Emily realized that Alex and Lucy would probably want to do something more than just hang around at her house on New Year's.

"Let's go see what's going on. We can drive around until we find something," Emily said.

Lucy nodded. "Yeah? That's what you want to do? Alex?"

Alex stood up. "Let's go," he said.

Waiting until Alex and Lucy were out of the room first, Emily slowly stood up. She turned off the light on her bedside table. She thought of Alex lying on top of her bed, and how it felt to put her hand on his forehead. She remembered sitting with Lucy in the kitchen. Alex and Lucy were two magnets, pulling her forward. She left the room, dark and empty.

Alex stopped in the bathroom again on the way out. Lucy and Emily went out to the garage and sat in the car, waiting for him to come outside.

"Is he okay?" Emily asked Lucy.

"He's just got a bad immune system. He catches everything."

"Like the flu and stuff?"

"Yeah," Lucy said, nodding. "Like the flu."

Lucy was watching her and she had been watching her all night.

"You're looking at me like I have something on my face."

"I'm not."

Alex came back out of the house and sat in the backseat. Lucy reached into her bag and produced a bottle of pills. Emily didn't know what they were.

"I brought these for you. You know, for your motion sickness," she said.

"Ixnay on the motion icknesssay," Alex said. He popped two pills in his mouth. He paused, as if considering, and then took two more.

Emily put her wallet in the front cup holder. It held some cash, a debit card, her driver's license, an emergency credit card that her grandmother had given her on her sixteenth birthday, her student ID card, and a handful of gift cards, several from her mom. Most were for clothing stores at the mall, but there were a few for fast food restaurants and coffee shops. Emily's mom sent them to her in the mail. It was a secondhand way of being with Emily in Victoria. Emily also had a voucher for a free round-trip ferry ride from Victoria to Vancouver to visit her mom, but she hadn't used it yet. She wasn't sure if she was going to.

Not while her grandmother was in the hospital, she knew that. And because she wouldn't think about after, what happened next, she couldn't think about a time when she would want to use it. It was tucked in a zippered compartment on the inside of her wallet, where she wouldn't come across it every time she had to take out cash.

She had spoken to her mom on the phone earlier in the week. Her mom had suggested she use the voucher to spend some of her Christmas holidays in Vancouver.

"You can come and visit me any time," her mom said. "We can do New Year's together."

"I'm not leaving Grandma here," Emily said. "Why don't you come to the island?"

"Because I have to work the next day, honey."

"So? You can do your work anywhere. You just need your computer."

"I'll think about it," her mom said. "I'll see what I can do."

Emily had known she wouldn't come.

"That thing's fat," Lucy said, lifting the wallet out of the cup holder and letting it fall from the height of a couple of inches.

"Jesus, Lucy, careful. That's Emily's," Alex said.

"It's fine," Emily said. "There's not really that much in there. It just looks like there is."

"Do you have any pictures or anything?" Lucy asked. "Our mom keeps basically an entire photo album in her wallet. She has baby pictures of me and Alex and then our school photos from every year since kindergarten. I don't know who she shows them to."

"Can you imagine Mom sitting at a table, taking out every single picture to show someone?" Alex said. "I bet they'd love that."

"I think I have a couple," Emily said. "You can check if you want."

Lucy opened the wallet and found three separate compartments inside: the one that held coins and change was zipped across the top, but the other two were left open. There were flaps on either side that opened up to hold Emily's cards. But tucked in one of the pockets by her change, Emily had a small collection of pictures she had forgotten about until Lucy mentioned them. She couldn't remember taking them out of her wallet to show people before. There wasn't anyone who didn't know all of the ins and outs of what she did and where she went and who she knew. There were no surprises and no secrets and no one who had just showed up in Emily's life. Not until Alex and Lucy.

"So, that's my grandma," Emily said, looking at the first picture Lucy was holding.

Before, Emily's grandfather died, he had walked around with his camera, snapping photos almost constantly. Emily had gotten used to the clicking sound of the photo being taken, the shutter speed and the aperture. The sounds were insect noises in the house. In this picture, her grandmother was sitting in a chair in the living room with that tasseled blanket thrown over her legs. It was a reminder that her grandmother hadn't always looked the way she looked now in the hospital. She was smiling at the camera. It must have been a sunny day because the house was bright and open. When it rained, they had to turn on every light. The grey swallowed everything.

"She looks really nice," Lucy said.

"She is," Emily said.

Alex looked at the picture for longer than his sister did. Emily noticed he glanced up at her and then back at the picture. He did it twice. She wondered if he was looking for some similarity between them.

"That one is of me and my mom, at the Tsawwassen ferry terminal, I think, when she was going back to Vancouver." They were almost the same height in that picture. Now Emily was taller by a couple of inches.

"So, she won't tell you who your dad is," Alex said.

"Alex," Lucy said, "stop asking Emily all this personal stuff."

"Sorry," Alex said. "But, it's just, if you don't want to tell us, you don't have to. It just seems like you don't mind."

"I don't," Emily said. "I just think it must be pretty boring for you guys, listening to me complain about stuff all night."

"You're not complaining," Alex said.

Lucy took out the next two photos. Emily had taken the first one of her grandparents on the day her grandfather had retired. He was dressed in a suit and her grandmother in a dress. They had gone out to dinner to celebrate. After, they had come home, packed their suitcases, and left from the harbor for a weeklong cruise. Emily's mom had come to stay with her for the week. She had been in grade six. The other picture had been taken during the week of the cruise. Emily's mom was in the kitchen, standing near the counter, stirring pancake batter in a large plastic bowl with a wooden spoon. Pancakes were the only thing her mom knew how to cook.

It was strange to see the moments that had been made to last, this handful of reminders of things that didn't represent the way it had been overall. These were the in-between, uncommon moments, the ones that were taken to be the things that had happened all the time.

"Emily, what's this one?" Lucy took out the last picture.

"Oh, God, I forgot that one was in there," Emily said.

"Is that the girl from the bowling alley?" Lucy asked.

"Veronica, right?" Alex said.

"Yeah, that's me and Veronica," Emily said.

"What are you doing?" Alex said.

"We were in a play together in grade ten. It was some weird thing that our drama teacher wrote himself."

"Good God," Lucy said.

"Well, yeah, basically," Emily said. "It was kind of awful. I mean, it was one of those symbolism things where everything has a meaning that's really different than the one you think it's going to be at first. But the problem was that all of the things were really personally symbolic to him so no one got it."

"What are you supposed to be?"

In the picture, Emily and Veronica had their faces painted blue. They were wearing tights and dresses and had glued on long false eyelashes. Emily had her arm around Veronica's shoulder. Veronica was smiling at the camera, holding her arm up in the air like she had won a prize.

"I have no idea. I can't even remember what that thing was about."

"Alex did a play one time." Lucy elbowed her brother. "Remember?"

"If you're talking about the Christmas plays we had to do in elementary school, those don't count."

"No, no, remember the one you had to do in front of the entire school?" Lucy said. When Alex still didn't show any recognition, Lucy turned to Emily and started explaining. "They asked for volunteers at some assembly. We were both in high school. I was in grade ten and Alex in grade eleven. This man asks for volunteers to act out some skit at the front of the gym, in front of everyone, and I see Alex's hand shoot up like his arm's on fire. I basically put my head in my hands because Alex embarrasses himself all the time," Lucy said. "It's his personal skill."

"It wasn't anything like memorizing lines," Alex said. "They just asked us to stand in this line and move our arms and stuff. I can't even remember what it was for. Can you?" he asked Lucy.

"No. I just remember you looked like an idiot."

"Thanks," Alex said.

Emily looked at Alex in the rearview mirror. He was leaning heavily on the car door. Emily wanted to prop him up and make him look well and healthy. She focused on the road and kept driving.

"So, it's just been you?" Alex said after a while.

"I guess," Emily said.

"Kind of lonely," Alex said.

"Yeah."

"Well, look. We're changing that," Lucy said.

"I guess you are," Emily said. "But what happens after tonight? I mean, what happens then?"

Alex looked at his hands. Lucy picked at her cuticles. Her fingernails cut into the skin, pulling it down until the small white half-moons of her nails were showing.

"Don't think about that," Alex said. "We don't like to think ahead a lot. We're going out. It's New Year's Eve. That's what happens next."

chapter*sixteen*

It started raining while they were driving. It wasn't anywhere near pouring yet, just a general dampness that
blurred the windshield. Emily drove in the loop of the city
that she could almost take without thinking. The loop had
started at her grandmother's house when she left with Alex
and Lucy half an hour before. It went down into Oak Bay
and hugged Beach Drive until it curved around the point
where the cruise ships came in to dock. She drove up Government Street to Foul Bay, and took the road past the University and then north to her grandmother's house. She was
about to start the loop again when she changed her mind
and took the familiar way back to the hospital.

She wasn't thinking about going back in. She knew they
couldn't. Visiting hours had ended and hospital staff and
security made sure that no one was on patient floors who
shouldn't be there. Emily had tried to stay at the hospital
overnight once. It had been early in her grandmother's stay
there, after the first week of her permanent living situation
in the geriatric ward. Emily hadn't slept all week. She had

been alone in the house after visiting hours ended, lying on her bed, staring at the ceiling, her body as straight as a board. She heard herself breathing. She felt her heart beat circles in her chest. This was how it was always going to be now. Emily alone in an empty house.

She couldn't tell her grandmother. She couldn't sit in the chair beside the hospital bed and say, "I can't go home. You don't know what it's like. It's so lonely." So instead, she waited until her grandmother fell asleep. Emily let her own head fall to the side, and she feigned her own sort of sleep, the kind that she hoped would inspire sympathy in which-ever nurse or doctor saw her in there, the kind that would get them to leave her alone until the morning.

But visiting hours ended, Emily's shoulder was given a rough shake, and she was sent outside and told to come back the next day. She took the bus home. Her grand-mother habitually gave her money for gas or to take a cab back home after the hospital, but Emily wasn't in that kind of hurry to get there. She didn't need the most direct way back to the house. She could take her time.

Emily turned the corner on the street and watched the hospital come into view. There were a few people moving in and out of the glass doors, those who had someone in emergency, or who were getting off shift, or taking a break outside.

"Why did you come this way?" Lucy asked. "Isn't this basically the last place we want to be tonight?"

"I don't know," Emily said, taken aback by the almost panicky tone of Lucy's voice. "I'm just driving around. I can go the other way if you want."

"Yeah, let's find somewhere else," Alex said.

"Your friend," Emily said, realizing her mistake in coming this way, "is he really sick?"

"He's pretty bad," Alex said.

Emily turned down the next street leading away from the hospital. She went back toward downtown. The rain was turning into damp fog that hugged the windshield and made it difficult to see. Emily turned on the defrost and opened her window a crack. A narrow stream of cold air slid into the car and started undoing the work of the sticky fog on the inside of the windows. Emily got back on the highway and took it in the direction of downtown. She cut through the center of the city until she was back on Beach Drive. She wondered what they were going to do. She couldn't drive around like this all night. Alex stared out the back window and Lucy alternated between looking through the windshield and the passenger window.

"Do you guys usually go out for New Year's?" Emily asked.

They answered at once. "Yes." "No."

"I do," Alex said. "I mean, the last couple of years there's always been something going on."

"Why not tonight?" Emily asked.

"I had to go to the hospital," Alex said. "And then I didn't feel like it. And then I met you." He was looking at her from the back seat. Emily, staring through the windshield, only looked at him from the corner of her eye, that peripheral perspective.

"But this is fun, right?" he said.

"Mom never lets me go anywhere," Lucy said. "So this is kind of great."

"For New Year's?" Emily asked.

"No, basically, in general. She's always, like, 'Lucy Hobbs, you come straight home from school and no stopping on the way.'"

"There's a reason for that, Lucy," Alex said.

"What?"

"You'd never come home."

"I would so," Lucy said.

"So, what?" Emily asked. "You usually stay home on New Year's?"

"I guess," Lucy said. "Me and Mom usually sit on the couch and watch those TV specials where they have people singing and dancing and recapping everything that happened over the year, and then that silver ball drops and Mom says, 'Okay, time for bed.'"

"It's not that bad," Alex said. "You like doing that."

"Sometimes," Lucy said.

Emily drove up Beach Drive, past Beacon Hill Park. When she was on the other side of it, she noticed the lights.

"Hey," she said. "What's going on over there?"

"I don't know." Alex craned his neck to see. "Do you want

to go and find out?"

Emily turned into the park. She drove by the petting zoo and the gardens. When Emily was younger and her mom came to visit from Vancouver, they'd all get into her grandmother's car and drive down to Beacon Hill Park. They'd buy hot dogs and milkshakes from the drive-thru and walk along the trails and paths. Her mom took her to the petting zoo once, a series of fenced-off sections for the goats, rabbits, and peacocks. A goat had grabbed the back of Emily's sweater and started eating the material from the hood. She had the sweater in her drawer at home, the square teeth marks still there.

"Look at that," Alex said. "I guess they're doing something for New Year's."

"We should go," Lucy said. "I mean, I really think we should."

Emily drove into the parking area. Three people in yellow vests were directing traffic. She was led down to the last row of cars, where there was one more parking space at the end. It was a tight turn, and Emily had to swoop in and around from a long way off in order to make it.

Lucy was the first one out of the car. She waited for her brother to get out, and then she held him by the arm and gave him a half-hug.

"See, isn't this perfect?" she said to him, as Emily locked the doors and pocketed her keys.

"It's great," Alex said. "Really."

There was a fair in the center of the park, with a midway and a Ferris wheel and covered booths. There was a band playing on the raised floor of a stage. Outside of that, there were people who had tarps and quilts spread out on the grass, sitting in groups and pairs.

"Em, do you like rides and stuff?" Lucy asked.

"Yeah," Emily said. "I kind of do."

They crossed the parking lot. The pavement was dark with rain, but it wasn't falling now. The air was chilled and damp. Even if it didn't rain, the way the moisture stayed in the air in front of them made their clothes feel constantly soggy. Emily hugged her arms around her chest and walked beside Alex and Lucy. They passed by two volunteers in bright vests and went inside.

As soon as they were through the barrier, it felt immediately warmer. Emily thought there had to be outdoor heaters inside.

"Where should we go first?" Emily asked.

"To get some tickets or something," Alex said. "I want to go on all the rides."

"Are you sure?" Lucy asked him. "Don't you usually get sick on those and stuff?"

Emily thought about the container of pills that Alex had been taking in the car, the ones for motion sickness. Her mom got sick driving in cars and from taking the ferry from the mainland to the island, so Emily had always thought of motion sickness as normal. Emily's grandfather used to tell her stories about her mother—doing things that she would never think to. Her mom learning how to drive a boat on the ocean. Her mom riding roller coasters at fairs in the British Columbia interior during the summers. Her mom driving in a van every winter, going from ski hill to ski hill across the Rocky Mountains. Carsick didn't translate into a general motion sickness. Emily knew that.

"Okay," Emily said. "Yeah, let's go on some rides and stuff. That sounds good."

They went toward a circular booth and tagged on to the end of a line eight people long. Lucy stood close to her brother. She held his elbow in her hand. Emily felt pressed in by people walking past her, knocking into her shoulder with their elbows, feet, and arms. There were children on their parents' shoulders and large dogs on leashes that extended a couple of feet in front of their owners. The gears and mechanisms of the rides screeched and creaked; the sound of air moving out of the way of the rides was a loud whooshing exhale. The line moved forward.

"Alex, what I'm saying is, I'm worried about you being sick," Lucy said, leaning against her brother's side. Emily had missed the beginning of the conversation.

"I'm fine," he told his sister. "Really."

"Rides make you sick?" Emily asked.

"No," Alex said. "They really don't."

"Now they might," Lucy said quietly.

"Lucy," Alex said, "look where we are. Look who we're

with." He looked over at Emily and gave her a grin. "Come on, isn't this exactly what you want to be doing?"

Lucy leaned into her brother, teetering on her feet. The line moved again and she went forward.

Emily watched their exchanges curiously, an outsider to their family. All the while, she felt as if there was a secret language being spoken. She had been let in, but clearly not to everything.

Alex bought them three wristbands so they could go on all the rides. Emily put her arm up on the counter of the small booth and felt the sticky paper press against her skin. Lucy and Alex did the same. Emily tried to pay, but Alex nudged her with his shoulder, his arms taking up the entire counter. His wallet was open, the ID card inched slightly out of position.

"You just get us some food or something," Alex said. "You know those things that are just dough fried in oil?"

"Donuts?" Emily said.

"Sort of," Alex said, grinning. "Only instead, they're the size of your head."

"You mean funnel cakes," Emily said.

"Basically it's fried fat," Lucy said. "So we should get some of that."

After Alex paid, they walked around the fairgrounds. Paths cut through one side to the other and connected with the midway, but Alex, Emily, and Lucy followed the circular route past all of the rides.

"As soon as anyone sees anything they want to go on," Alex said, "just say something."

"There," Lucy said. "I want a candy apple."

"What about a ride first?" Alex asked.

"But the apple things are right here. We'll probably never find them again."

"I'll get it," Emily said.

She went up to the counter and picked out two candy apples and a caramel apple. There were lines everywhere, coming out of the booths and the rides, and one formed behind Emily while she paid for the apples. She took them back to Alex and Lucy. They stood so close together, their shoulders touched. The way Lucy looked at her brother, Emily couldn't not see the concern in the way the middle of her forehead wrinkled down to the bridge of her nose.

"Those look amazing," Lucy said, taking the red candy apple. Emily held onto the other and Alex took the caramel.

"That has to be the most unhealthy thing to do in the entire history of the world," Lucy said, as her brother peeled the caramel off the apple in one long piece. His jaw worked up and down, straining at the side.

"It's good," he said through a mouthful. "I don't need to be healthy anyway."

The lines for the rides all seemed too long when they walked past them, so Lucy and Emily stood in lines for food and brought the things they had purchased back to Alex. They sat at a long picnic table and ate pieces of fried dough and kettle corn and corn dogs off a stick. Emily bought a large cup of Coke and put it on the table between the three of them, three white straws poking up from the plastic lid.

"Are we really going on rides after this?" Emily asked.

"Yeah," Alex said, smiling. "Of course we are."

The entire time, the fair became busier and busier, with more people coming in through the front entrance.

"We better go stand in a line if we want to go on something," Alex said.

"Yeah, well, let's do something easy since we just stuffed our faces," Lucy said. "No one ever throws up on the Ferris wheel, right?"

The Ferris wheel was opposite the entrance, tall, spinning, and with its axles all lit up with blinking lights that chased each other around the circumference of the wheel. They slid into a bucket seat, Alex and Lucy sitting on either side of Emily, their elbows pressing into hers. The Ferris wheel turned and lifted them up into the air, swinging around in a circle and clearing the very top.

"Alex? Are you okay?" Lucy asked, leaning over Emily.

"I'm fine," he said. He shrugged his shoulders at her. "Don't I look fine?"

He didn't look as bad as he had earlier. The circles under his eyes had been growing more prominent all night, but the way he was looking at his sister with this everything-is-okay-why-would-you-think-it-was-any-other-way   face made Emily think the same thing: what would be wrong?

"So, the last time we were on a Ferris wheel was in Alberta," Lucy said. "We had to go to Calgary to visit Mom's relatives and they were all, like, 'Well, let's take these west coasters to the Calgary Stampede.'"

"Was it fun?"

"Alex is allergic to horses," Lucy said. "And it's basically just a big rodeo with a couple of rides in there, also."

"It was fun," Alex amended. "We went on everything."

"Including the Ferris wheel," Lucy said.

"I haven't even been out of British Columbia," Emily said. "And you guys just drive to Alberta? That's kind of nice."

"Yeah, we're maybe overselling ourselves on that," Alex said. "We go to Alberta maybe once a year. That's it."

"That's still more than me," Emily said.

"Well, next time, you can come with us," Lucy said.

Emily laughed, but Lucy just looked at her earnestly.

"You're serious?" she said. "You just met me and you're inviting me to visit your family."

"Yeah, well, we like you," Lucy said.

They were quiet for a few minutes, sitting in their seats as the Ferris wheel went all the way around. It stopped for more time than it was actually in motion, but Emily liked looking out at everything, all of the people at the fair below her, standing, walking, eating, talking, their colorful clothes making them look like a quilt spread over the ground. If she looked up, straight in front of her, she could see out over the entire ocean. It was inky black in the nighttime, but she knew it was still there, just out on the other side of Beach Drive. For one overwhelming moment, Emily thought, this was home. This was the city where she lived. She could see almost all of it. She didn't think she'd feel that way if she were here alone. If she were anywhere alone. But pressed between Alex and Lucy, Emily felt like this was the place where she belonged.

The Ferris wheel went back to the ground. They got off. Lucy and Alex stood together and looked at Emily. She scuffed her feet against the flattened grass, warming her toes inside her shoes.

"What do you think?" she said. "More rides?"

Lucy and Alex exchanged a look.

"More rides," Lucy said, smiling. "Come on, before the lines get long again."

Alex and Emily walked behind Lucy. Lucy kept on turning to look behind her, as if she were checking up on their progress. When she saw that they were there, and fine, she looked ahead again, navigating through the crowds and carving out a skinny path for Alex and Emily to follow.

"I like your sister," Emily told Alex.

Alex smiled. "It's nice doing this. For both of us, really."

"Yeah, well, for me, too."

After that, they went from ride to ride to ride. Emily had only an impression of blinking lights, of light smeared across the dark sky, trailing in long, snaky patterns. Of all the rides so far, there was nothing that flipped them upside down and nothing that spun too fast or was too much. Not for Emily, at least. The three of them squeezed in together, in seats meant for two.

For the first time in months, Emily didn't think about anything. She didn't let her mind go toward the things that she usually spent her time on. She wasn't at home or at the hospital or at school. She was just at the fair with Alex and Lucy. She was just going from one ride to the next without any idea of how long they were going to stay or when the night would end.

Every once in a while, she would have to help Alex get into a booth or a car or a seat. Emily and Lucy would stand on either side of him and help for a moment when he looked unbalanced where he stood. Emily tried to exchange a look with Lucy when it happened. She'd look over and ask for an explanation without asking directly. But Lucy avoided looking back. She would just sit in the seat, Alex now in the middle between them, and wait for the ride to start.

Emily loved the Tilt-A-Whirl. She loved being flung around in circles, knowing there was nothing she could do except grip the metal bar that cut across her thighs and feel her heart turn in her chest. The lights spread out and flashed through the dark sky. Their backs slid against the plastic, jarring them into one another. Long stretches of music streamed in and out of hearing, cut off when their compartment pulled to the left or the right as the ride turned and turned.

When Alex gripped the bar, Emily thought it was because of the big spin that happened before the ride was over, the last push and pull in opposite directions. She thought it was because of the ride.

"Hey, hey, hey," Lucy said. "What's happening?"

The ride kept spinning. Emily turned. Lucy's hand gripped Alex's arm and his knuckles were white and pale. The sounds and the spinning swelled and made a bubble around Alex and Lucy, separating them from the rest of it all. Emily's head spun. She leaned into the bar and tried to keep the two things separate: what was happening inside their compartment and what was happening outside.

"Stop the ride, stop the ride," Lucy shouted. She leaned out of the front of the booth and shouted louder. The ride operator couldn't hear her. Emily called with her a few times, not sure what was happening but having the overwhelming feeling that it was important.

Finally the ride stopped. Lucy threw the bar off of their laps.

"Help me," she said to Emily, as she held onto Alex's arm.

Emily and Lucy got Alex out of the compartment. He was stiff and his eyes glazed, and his face was pale. He took small steps across the ground. Emily and Lucy half-lifted and half-carried him onto the grass.

Alex's eyes were huge and dark. He was somewhere else,

Emily thought, not here. He leaned over and threw up onto the grass.

"Alex, Alex," Lucy said, rubbing his back. "You're okay, you're okay."

Emily didn't know if she should help or stay back. "I'll go get some water," she said.

As she jogged away from Lucy and Alex, he was still throwing up. He hadn't even taken a breath. Emily's heart raced as she found a food vendor. She waited in line, at the back, before deciding that she didn't have the time. She went up to the front of the line and said, "My friend's sick, I'm sorry. He needs water."

And still she had to wait, her heart beating hard in her chest, wishing the man inside the concession stand would go faster.

chapter*seventeen*

"Alex, Alex, okay, we have to stop this. We have to stop this now," Lucy said. She rubbed Alex's back. She kneeled beside him in the grass and tried to come up with a way to stop him from throwing up. There were people watching, but they weren't doing anything. She didn't know why it was taking Emily so long to get a glass of water.

That helplessness she felt watching her brother being sick at the fair had threaded throughout the timeline of Alex's cancer. The times when there was nothing she could do about the way he was feeling and the things that were happening to him. It manifested and built up when she watched him get worse and look worse and feel worse. She couldn't say anything to him or to her parents. They all felt the same about it. Saying it out loud didn't make it better. Instead, Lucy's helplessness would release through ways she couldn't control.

Like at the Homecoming dance at her school. She had gone with Stephanie. Alex thought he was going to go with them, but that plan fell apart the moment he learned that his cancer was back. Lucy and Stephanie still went, but they felt the hole in between them, the gap in the way it was supposed to be.

That night, Lucy didn't feel herself from the moment she looked at the deflated Homecoming dress in her closet. By the time Stephanie arrived out front in the limousine that seemed too big for just the two of them, she was wishing the night were already over. Still, they drove to the dance and went up to the doors of the school. A teacher Lucy didn't know took their tickets and ripped off the edges in case they wanted to keep the other half as a souvenir. Stephanie tucked hers back into her purse.

It was dark in the gym, where the dance was. There were streamers hanging from the ceiling and letters spelling out "Homecoming" on the walls. There was a place set up where they could get their picture taken. Stephanie made a beeline for the photographer but Lucy said, "Maybe later," and kept walking.

The lights were going. They were all different colors and there was a DJ at the front of the gym. Someone had set up a table with pop and snacks and bags of chips, and when Stephanie went over to the table, Lucy went with her. There were people from their classes, and then there were people in grades eleven and twelve. Lucy felt small in her dress.

It was automatic, the start of the questions. "Why isn't your brother back at school yet? "Are you bringing his homework home for him every day?" Is he getting any better?" "What's going to happen to him?" Lucy could usually field the questions. She could give one-word answers or form a sentence that would placate someone for the few minutes she needed to find a way to extricate herself from the conversation. But Alex's absence made all the questions unanswerable.

Lucy's heart started thumping and the music seemed to get louder in the gym. Stephanie was talking to someone else and hadn't heard the question that Lucy had been asked, so she couldn't know what it felt like to fall apart on the inside. For Lucy, it was that big dying thing. It was finding out Alex's cancer was back and there was nothing Lucy could do about it. It was being in the middle of all of the people who didn't have a reason for feeling the way she felt. They didn't have brothers who had cancer, who were supposed to come to Homecoming but couldn't.

"Hey, Lucy, are you okay?"

"I'm fine." She lurched toward the table where there were plastic glasses and she filled one up with water and tried to drink it quickly, to wash away the lump in her throat.

"Enjoying the dance?" Mr. Brummell asked as she gulped the water down.

All of the flashing lights in the gym were dancing off his face.

"It's okay," Lucy lied. "I'm fine."

"Haven't seen you in class lately."

Lucy shrugged. She had missed an entire week of English

class. She hadn't meant to; it had just happened. She went home and sat on the couch with Alex instead and they watched movies. Sweat dripped down her back. She didn't think Mr. Brummell knew what was happening.

"You're going to have to do something, Lucy. Lots of late assignments to catch up on."

"Yeah. I will. Look, I've got to go." As she turned away, some of the water in her glass sloshed up and across her dress.

She couldn't see Stephanie in the crowd. It killed her that she couldn't find her. Lucy was a shaking ball of anxiety. She needed to get to the washroom. She tried to leave.

"Sorry, you'll have to use the ones in the gym. School's off limits."

It was Bonnie, Lucy's gym teacher. When Lucy had started skipping school, gym had been the first class to go. They had had "a talk" about her attendance that created an awkwardness between them, one that had persisted and grown over time.

"I really need to leave," Lucy said.

"Then go back out the front doors. But once you leave, you're not allowed back in."

Lucy's hand felt disconnected from her brain. Her glass of water went right into Bonnie's face, giving Lucy just enough time to slip past her and out into the hallway.

She was running, but not breathing, and she was getting lightheaded. She couldn't hear Bonnie anymore, but she had a feeling that Bonnie was shouting after her. Lucy's ears were a wall and nothing was getting through. There were little spots in front of her eyes. She reached out for the wall and her fingers found the fire alarm and she pulled.

Someone in the gym screamed. After the first scream, several followed. Lucy kept going down the hall, away from the pulled fire alarm. She could hear the sound of the doors opening outside. She was sweating. She didn't know if she was even breathing anymore.

"Lucy? What are you doing in here? They're evacuating the gym."

It was Mr. Brummell, checking the hallway for left-behind students. Bonnie was with him and as soon as Lucy saw her, she felt all the life drain out of her. Her blood pressure hit the ground. She leaned against the wall, vibrating in place.

Bonnie made a beeline for Lucy. Mr. Brummell took a step forward to get between them.

"Hey, hey, Bonnie," Mr. Brummell said, keeping them apart. "Can you help the rest of the students get out of the gym?"

Bonnie stood there for a second, glaring at Lucy before she backed out of the hallway.

Mr. Brummell sighed and pointed to the exit. "Come on, Lucy. The fire department's on its way."

But Lucy just sank into the wall. "There's no fire," she said.

"It doesn't matter if there's a fire or not. The alarm went off."

"I pulled it," Lucy said.

Sweat was just dripping off her. She could feel it on her forehead and down her back.

"You okay?" he asked her. "You're not looking so great."

He led her to his English classroom. The fire alarm was still going. The sirens from the fire trucks were just starting to get loud. When he unlocked the classroom, Lucy sat down at a desk and tried to breathe again. It was as if she had to think about it, the in and out of breathing.

Mr. Brummell brought her a bottle of water and then he sat on his desk. Lucy noticed Gandalf in the poster on the wall behind him, all tall and strong and insistent about the passing thing.

She wiped her hair out of her eyes and realized that they were wet. She sniffed a big gob of snot and phlegm into her nose. "My brother's cancer came back," she said. "He had leukemia and then it went into remission. And then he got kind of bad again but I didn't know how bad, and I really believed he'd get better until he went into the hospital again and they told him it was terminal. He's not going to get better."

After a moment, Mr. Brummell said, "You just found this out?"

Lucy nodded. She held her hands together tightly on her lap.

Mr. Brummell sighed. Lucy stared at Gandalf. It was better than looking down at her dress, stained with tears and sweat and spilled water. Her heartbeat was starting to get back to normal and she was taking shaky breaths that sounded like the best thing she'd heard all night.

"You like *Lord of the Rings*?" Mr. Brummell asked.

She shrugged. "I guess that's an understatement."

"Really?"

"Yeah, it's kind of my favorite thing. Alex bought me my first Tolkien book when I was in middle school. I get a little obsessive about it, especially now."

"Because of your brother?"

"Yeah."

"You know who my favorite is?"

Lucy didn't feel like making conversation, but she went along anyway. "Who?"

"Sam. The unsung hero of *Lord of the Rings*."

"Yeah, Sam's okay."

"No," Mr. Brummell said. "Sam's *great*. Maybe he's not the one who the story is about, but he's there for everything. And you know, he helps Frodo through the quest. You take Sam away and do you think there'd be a happy ending?"

"Probably not," Lucy said. "But Frodo could probably do it on his own."

Mr. Brummell shook his head. "I don't think so, Lucy. I think that's the most important part, that Sam's there the whole time. And he does everything he can to help, but at the end of it, it's not his story. He goes in and out of it, but in the end, he gets left behind. It goes on without him."

"Yeah," Lucy said. "But that's the worst part. That he gets left behind and Frodo goes off with the elves."

"But Sam stays," Mr. Brummell says. "And he makes his own story."

They sat in the classroom for a few more minutes. Lucy scraped her hair back off her neck and the outside breeze came in and cooled her down.

"I'm not Sam," she finally said.

Mr. Brummell shrugged his shoulders. "I'm not saying you are."

"I mean, I guess we have things in common, but I'm not Sam."

Mr. Brummell stood up. He peeled off the poster from beside the blackboard and rolled it up tightly. He snapped it up with an elastic band and reached out across the desk. Lucy took it from him and held it in her hands, still sweaty with anxiety.

"You need me to call your parents to get you home?"

"No," Lucy said. "Stephanie's out there. She's probably wondering where I am."

"Make sure you find her."

They went out the door and he turned off the lights and locked up the classroom again.

"You're going to be okay," Mr. Brummell said.

Lucy nodded. She held onto the poster. It crossed her chest like a sash.

The fire alarm was just one of those things that happened

when the sadness and uncertainty took over. The uncertainty about what would happen next, the certainty about the fact that Alex wasn't going to come out of this one. Now, seeing Alex collapsed in the grass after the Tilt-A-Whirl ride, Lucy felt that anxiety and sickness take over, funneling like a cloud of energy that needed to find a release. She could see Emily standing at a concession stand and for one moment she thought Emily was the reason her brother had gotten so bad. Lucy hadn't wanted it to go like this. She wanted Alex to do what he had to do, tell Emily what he wanted to tell her, and then go back to the hospital. As much as it had been nice so far, the three of them, she still wanted Alex to herself.

"Alex," Lucy said, scrambling for the few pills that she had left in her pocket. They had been collecting what they thought they might need for this one night. Still, it wasn't very much, because Alex couldn't save that much of his medication over the last week. He needed all of it.

"Alex," she said again, because repeating his name was the only thing she could do. She watched him try to breathe. He hadn't taken a breath in so long. Alex spluttered and coughed. Lucy's heart beat fast and hard.

"I'm okay," he said, eventually, wiping his hand across his mouth. "I think that's it."

Lucy led him away from the vomit. She laid him down in the grass and sat beside him. Emily still wasn't back, and Alex had to swallow two pills without water. He couldn't wait. His Adam's apple bobbed gratefully as he swallowed them down.

"It's time to go back," Lucy said.

Alex shook his head, his eyes closed tight.

"You're getting worse. You're not going to make it a lot further."

"I can still go for a little while."

"I'm really worried. I really am. I know you want to do this for Emily; I know you've been thinking about it for a while, but Alex, I'm scared."

Alex just smiled. "Lucy, it's not just for Emily. It's for you, too."

Her heart squeezed.

"It's so that you have someone when I'm gone."

"Alex, I'm going to be fine. I really am. We just need to get you better. We have to get you to the hospital to do that."

"No," he said. "Not the hospital. It was just a mistake to go on that last ride after everything else. That's all it was. Just a mistake. I want to keep going."

"Going where?" Lucy asked.

"Justin's house," Alex said. "We should spend New Year's with him. He told us about the party weeks ago, right? He'll want us to go."

"Justin won't care if we're there or not."

"I want to go there," Alex said. "We should tell her there."

Lucy didn't want to take Alex to another place, but if she was going to choose somewhere, she thought Justin's would probably be the best. When Alex had first been diagnosed with leukemia, Justin had been the only person outside of the immediate family who came over to the house to visit. Justin wouldn't stay there, though. He would help Alex get packed up and drive him over to his house across the city. He did it to get Alex out of the house. And when Alex came back, Lucy always noticed how much better he seemed than when he was stuck at home all day without anyone to talk to. If there was any place they should go tonight, it was Justin's.

There was only one thing still bothering Lucy.

"We can't just tell her here? We have to tell her something. After this?"

"I don't want to tell her here," Alex said. "I want to tell her when we're all together. Can't you see why Justin's house is a good idea?"

Lucy thought about it, and she couldn't find anything wrong with going to their cousin's. His parents were always gone for New Year's. He was having a party, and while that was probably not a good place to tell Emily, they would make Justin's work because they had to. They had to get Alex sitting down or lying down and on his way to feeling better. He had to get out of the cold and the damp. Aside from taking him back to the hospital, Lucy couldn't think of another way.

"Okay," she said. "Okay. Look, here she comes."

chapter*eighteen*

"Emily! Over here!" Lucy called.

Emily looked for the place Lucy's voice had come from. She crossed the narrow patch of grass and went over to where Alex was lying on the ground. Lucy was on her knees beside him. A woman with a baby was standing over them both, but Lucy seemed to be waving her away.

"We're fine, everything's okay," Lucy told her. "Thanks, though."

The woman left, uncertainly, and Emily knelt beside Lucy and held out the cup of water.

"What happened?" she asked. "Are you okay?"

"I'm fine," Alex said, his eyes closed.

"Was it the rides?" Emily asked.

"Yeah," Alex said. "It was."

Lucy was staring at Emily. It was a kind and sympathetic

look, a you-don't-even-know look. She took the water from
Emily and held it out to Alex.

"It wasn't the rides," Lucy said.

"Lucy," Alex said.

"Here, Emily brought you this," Lucy said, handing him
the water. He moved until he was propped on his elbow,
able to take a drink. "We should tell her."

"Tell me what?"

"Alex isn't sick because of the rides. He's sick because he
has cancer."

It didn't change anything, at first. For Emily, cancer was
something that happened, that people hid well until it dis-
appeared or until chemotherapy worked.

"You weren't visiting someone in the hospital," she said.

"No," Alex said.

"*I* was," Lucy said. "So we didn't lie about that. I was visiting him."

"You're supposed to be at the hospital," Emily said.

"Yeah."

"Then let's get you back there."

Alex shook his head. He took a few sips of water from the
plastic cup. Lucy put her hand on his shoulder. She didn't
tell him he should go to the hospital. She didn't say anything. Emily didn't understand why they would be out here,
where he was looking worse than he had when she first met
him, when he could be better in the hospital.

"It's my last big night out," Alex said. "It's not over yet."

"What do you mean?"

"It's my last night to do something like this. To actually live it out and do anything that I still have left to do."

"Alex," Emily said, but she couldn't find the words that came next.

"Our cousin, he's having a party tonight. We told him we might go. He knows all about the cancer. It's a good place to go."

Emily looked between the two siblings. Everything that had happened, it was all laid out between them.

"Lucy? You think this is okay?" Emily asked her.

Lucy sat back on her heels, one hand on her brother's shoulder. She squeezed.

"I think we should go to the party," she said.

Emily didn't know what to say. Her grandmother was in the hospital and she was going to stay in the hospital. But Emily thought that if her grandmother had wanted to leave, had wanted to go home or to her favorite restaurant to see the ocean before the end, she would take her. She stood up and wiped her hands down her jeans.

"Okay," she said. "Let's go to your cousin's."

chapter*nineteen*

Knowing Alex was sick changed nothing and every-thing. Emily couldn't stop checking on him, turning to look and make sure he was okay.

There was nowhere to park in front of Justin's house, so Emily circled around, hoping someone would leave.

"Em, it's fine, just park around the block," Alex said.

"I don't want you to have to walk far," she said.

"I'm fine," Alex said. "I'm feeling better now."

Emily was in the front seat alone. Lucy was in the back with her brother. Emily looked at them through the rear-view mirror as she drove. Lucy watched her brother, her eyes glassy and wet. She wasn't crying, but every once in a while her face would screw up tight and she'd sniff loudly. Alex stared out the window. Emily didn't know how to read him. It wasn't that he was happy, it was more that he was content. This is where he wanted to be. Lucy didn't want him to be here, but he wanted to be here. That tension in the backseat was unmistakable.

After watching him at the fair, bent over in the grass and throwing up without stopping, Emily felt like she couldn't let it get like that again. And then she realized that it wasn't up to her the way his cancer manifested. She couldn't do anything.

At first she wondered if she should take him back to the hospital. It didn't matter what Alex and Lucy said, Emily thought she should drive back there and take them upstairs to the room in the cancer ward and leave Alex there to get better. She knew that was the thing she should do. That was the thing that, more than anything else, needed to be done. But she couldn't imagine the night ending now, less than two hours before midnight. Part of her didn't want it to end. And maybe more importantly, Alex didn't. So she kept driving.

Emily helped Alex get out of the backseat and locked the doors. On the sidewalk, he walked normally. Lucy hovered by his shoulder in case he needed help.

"I'm fine," he said. "You don't need to do this. I'm fine."

"Alex, just let us help, okay?" Lucy said.

"I'm fine," he repeated.

They were walking very close together and Emily felt a slight pressure on her side as Alex leaned against her. She linked her arm in his as she navigated the sidewalk. Her mouth opened and gulped like a fish as she tried to say out loud the words, *Are you okay?* But something stopped her, a nudging at the back of her head that was a reminder of the number of times she had already asked him tonight. Instead, she held on tighter and kept them moving.

Emily's cell phone vibrated in her pocket and the noise was loud on the quiet street. The only reason she didn't reach into her pocket and turn it off was because of her grandmother. If something happened at the hospital, she needed to know. The vibration sent a shock up and down her thigh like the fizzle in a glass of lemonade. It made her lips purse together tightly.

Alex stopped on the sidewalk. "Em, I think your phone's ringing," he said.

"I know."

"You don't want to answer it?"

She removed the phone from her pocket and checked the caller ID. It was the same as it had been all night.

"Not really," she said. "It's my mom." She took Alex's arm again and they kept on walking.

"And you don't want to talk to her?"

"No." The quiet was changed by the words they spoke, the ones that left things hanging in the air between them. "She hasn't visited in a while," Emily said. "It's been long enough that it's hard to answer her phone calls, to listen to her ask stupid questions about my night, like I should drop every-thing because she's decided to care. She was supposed to be here for Christmas and she wasn't. She was supposed to come tonight and she hasn't."

"Where's she been?" Alex asked.

"Vancouver," Emily said. "That's it." Alex had slowed down and Emily held onto his hand. It was so cold.

"Your mom, she sounds sort of interesting," Lucy said.

"I guess that's the nice way to put it."

"Did she used to live here, though? In Victoria?"

"She grew up here," Emily said.

They stopped in front of Justin's house, where Christmas lights were strung around the eaves and front porch.

"Here, can we help you up the stairs, at least?" Emily asked. Alex was standing on the sidewalk, looking at her. Lucy, too. They did that, occasionally, and Emily would turn to see them both standing there, waiting for her to say or do something.

"Sure," Alex said eventually. Emily held onto his arm. They walked up the stairs and waited. Lucy didn't knock on the door. She put her hand on the doorknob and turned. Lucy and Alex kicked off their shoes and threw their jackets on the chair in the entranceway. Emily did the same, just more slowly.

She was tucking her gloves into the pocket of her jacket when a boy walked into the front entranceway from down the hall. He walked purposefully, his feet bare and the sleeves of his sweater rolled up to his elbows.

"You guys just get here?" he asked.

"Yep," Lucy said. "Hey, Justin."

Justin wasn't very tall. He had thick shoulders and a prominent collarbone. His hair was long and curling and it covered up his high forehead. It went all the way down past his eyebrows.

"I thought you were supposed to be in the hospital," he said. "Got a couple of calls tonight from your parents. They're looking for you."

"We'll call them later," Lucy said.

"You need me to take you back the hospital or something, just make sure you tell me before I'm blackout drunk."

"Yeah, I'll try," Alex said.

"Really, man, you okay?"

"I'm really okay. I'm going to find the bathroom."

"Use the one upstairs," Justin said.

Emily fiddled with the pocket of her jacket, folding and refolding her gloves while Alex and Lucy caught up with their cousin.

"Who's this?" Justin asked, looking over at her.

"This is Emily," Lucy said. "She didn't have any plans for New Year's."

"Glad I can let you use my house for your partying needs," Justin said.

"Are there a lot of people coming?" Lucy asked him.

"Yeah, I guess. The ferry gets in from Vancouver in a couple of minutes and then a bunch of people are going to drive here. Everyone else is upstairs."

"Anyone we know?" Lucy asked.

"Doubt it," Justin said.

They went through the hallway and to the kitchen. Alex's footsteps were loud on the stairs and Emily could hear him moving around right over her head, clumping and clomping like his feet were in the walls.

"Lucy," Emily said.

Lucy jumped up onto the kitchen counter and slid across. It was a very long counter and a very large kitchen. Emily thought she could fit the first floor of her grandparents' house in there and still have room left over.

"Is Alex going to be able to make it until midnight?" Emily asked.

"I don't know," Lucy said. "It was his idea to do this. You know, it's not bad, considering. When Alex got diagnosed, he used to spend hours online, looking up these stories from other people who were his age and had leukemia. He'd just lie on the couch with his laptop on his chest and read that stuff for hours. He told me that a lot of people, when they knew things were going to get bad, they just left. If they were in the hospital, they asked someone to get them out. If they were at home, they'd leave. Some group of close friends would travel with them. Someone wants to see Paris, they all go to Paris."

"Even though they're sick?"

"It's touch and go, I guess," Lucy said. "It's a lot of strain, going out like this, but Alex has basically looked like this for the last month. It's just this constant not-okayness that he has. I don't think he's telling me how he's really doing."

"So this is his runaway thing?" Emily asked.

"Yeah," Lucy said.

"Why here?"

Lucy shrugged but stared at the ground. "I guess there's something he wants to do."

Lucy opened the cupboard above her head and removed a box of crackers. She pulled out four square crackers and put them beside her on the counter. She pushed them around until the sides joined together to make one big square. She didn't seem very interested in eating them. Emily crossed the kitchen to open the fridge. She was looking for ginger ale or Sprite, something that was supposed to be sipped slowly with a straw from a warm cup. She wondered if it would help Alex feel better.

Lucy was checking her cell phone, staring at the small screen for a moment too long before shoving it back into her pocket.

"Our parents are looking for him. For us, I guess," Lucy said. "My phone's been going all night."

"You can't call them?"

"You can't call your mom?" Lucy asked, her eyebrows arching.

Upstairs, someone turned on a stereo. There wasn't much music to filter down the stairs into the kitchen, just the left-behind bass that vibrated through the ceiling. Emily shut the fridge.

Still on the countertop, Lucy was twisting a strand of hair around her finger and staring off into a middle space. She pulled at her hair and brought it in front of her face, staring it at cross-eyed. Emily hated to think about how she must look. She hadn't seen herself in a mirror since leaving her house. That was before the rain and the fair. It seemed like longer than just a couple of hours ago.

"You want to try and fix my hair?" Lucy asked her.

"It looks fine."

"Yeah, but it'll give us something to do until Alex comes back."

"What do we need?"

"There's probably a curling iron somewhere. I'll look around down here if you check upstairs."

The sound of music and laughing upstairs made Emily's chest tighten. She was a stranger here, even with Lucy and Alex. Still, she nodded, left the kitchen, and headed upstairs.

chapter*twenty*

I n the bathroom at Justin's, Alex took off his clothes and tried to wipe off the vomit. He got into the shower. The water fell over him, which was just what he needed after the fair. He made it as hot as he could stand it, the steam fogging the mirror and windows and leaving him reflectionless.

He hadn't wanted to tell Emily about his cancer. Still, it was the more straightforward of the two secrets he had.

Since around the time the phone calls started, Alex had known something was going to change.

The change came in the form of a 104-degree fever. Alex had never been afraid to drive with one of his parents before, but the way his mom drove him to the hospital was worse than the feeling of fever. The car rocked back and forth on its wheels every time she turned the corner, and there were a lot of corners between their house and the hospital.

"He's got a fever," Alex's mom explained to Dr. Davies. "His sister came home with the flu."

"We'll keep him here for the day. He can go home if his fever breaks by the evening."

"I should stay with you," Alex's mom said, sitting down on the edge of his bed.

"I'll be fine," Alex said.

After she left, Alex went down to the hospital cafeteria. He was still dressed in his street clothes and he blended in with the visitors. He wanted to get something to eat before Dr. Davies pumped him full of the medication that would make him nauseous. He sat in a booth near the windows. The heat from the open vents on the floor warmed his feet inside his shoes.

"I can't come back yet. I'm sorry."

Alex's head snapped up. The woman's voice behind him was familiar. He looked around. In a booth behind him sat a woman the same age as his mom and across from her was a woman as old as *her* mom would be. Alex couldn't see the old woman, just her hair, sitting on top of her head like a cotton ball. But he could see the younger woman and she had a face that he didn't want to look at for very long. It was very beautiful. It was the kind of face that sucked you in until you weren't just looking. You were staring.

"She misses you," said the old woman.

"Does she?"

"You're her mother."

"I always figured she was happier with you and Dad than she was with me."

"You know that's not true."

"Sometimes."

Things were slowly clicking together. Synapses did their snapping thing, their cracking thing, until they joined and made sense. The voice was familiar because Alex had heard it a lot recently. On the phone, when the woman had called. The woman looking for his dad. He listened harder.

"She doesn't know I'm home yet."

"She'll know soon."

"Not from you."

"Of course from me, Kate," the older woman said. Her voice was tired and slow.

"I'm not ready to do this yet."

"You're already looking for him. You're already doing this."

For a while it sounded like silence. It took Alex a long time to realize that they were still talking, just too quietly for him to hear. Alex wasn't moving or breathing, but he still couldn't hear what they were saying.

Eventually there was a scuffle along the floor as they rose to leave.

"I should get you back upstairs," the woman called Kate said.

"This isn't fair to Emily."

"I know."

Alex sat in the cafeteria after they left. His legs were heavy and his head was burning. He couldn't eat anything. His head was somewhere else, going wherever it needed to in order to figure out the two women who maybe both knew his father.

When he got back to his room, Dr. Davies was waiting. He told Alex he couldn't leave the hospital, that he wouldn't be going home again. He was told what that meant.

Alex stood in the shower for a few more minutes before he figured he should go downstairs. He turned off the water.

The two women in the hospital had led him to Emily. Stuck up in the hospital without anything to do but lie in bed all day, Alex had gone looking for the old woman from the cafeteria. He had found her on the geriatrics floor. And in that room was Emily, sitting on a hard-backed wooden chair, visiting. And Alex had started to wonder.

chapter*twenty-one*

Emily stopped at the top of the stairs, trying to determine which room the music was coming from. She walked toward a door, cracked open just enough to let out the light from inside. She could see the corner of a tiled floor of what was probably a washroom. Emily always thought that washrooms were safe places in a house full of people.

She pushed open the door, but the moment her fingers touched the handle, she knew she'd done something wrong.

Alex was standing in front of the mirror in the bathroom, his shirt off and his hair wet. A damp towel lay on the floor and he tripped over it when he noticed Emily watching.

"Sorry," she said, hurriedly shutting the door behind her.

When the heavy door separated the two of them, she felt her heart racing. It wasn't that Alex had been halfway through getting dressed again after a shower, or that she had walked in on him in a place he should be alone.

Instead, it was the way his chest had looked in the glare of the bathroom lights. It was a very pale white, spotted all over with bruises. Their edges were uneven and rippled, colored grey and blue and purple and green.

She heard the click of the door. Alex came out of the bathroom, wearing his shirt but not his sweater. When he got close enough she could smell body wash and shampoo.

"God, I'm sorry, Alex."

"It's okay."

"No," she said. "I should've knocked or something. I didn't know."

"Hey," he said, and she felt his hand on her arm. "It's not a big deal."

The electric feeling subsided and when Emily looked up, Alex seemed just the same as he had been all night. There was a reason for the bruises. He had leukemia. He wasn't going to be okay.

"What happened to Lucy?" Alex asked eventually.

"She's waiting for me. I'm looking for a curling iron."

"There's probably one in here," he said.

They both squeezed into the bathroom. Alex picked up the towel from the floor and hung it up on the back of the door. Emily bent down and opened the cupboard beneath the sink. She could feel Alex moving behind her, opening the closet and shuffling things around. Her knees were creaking as she leaned forward and her heels felt thick.

"I found it," Alex said, his voice muffled by the inside of

the closet. Emily went to stand up, but her feet slipped out from under her and she fell back instead, landing on the soft, damp bath mat.

Alex sat down beside her. He held out the curling iron, the cord wrapped tightly around the barrel. It started to unravel when Emily had it in her hands. The metal prongs of the power plug caught in the bath mat.

"It's probably a good idea to sit now." Alex reached his arms out behind him and leaned on them heavily. "I'd say that in twenty minutes, it's going to be insane."

"You think that many people are coming?"

"Justin's pretty ... popular," he conceded, but it didn't sound like the right word, just the one that had been the first available.

"I can tell."

They were quiet. Emily twisted the curling iron between her palms.

"Em, at your house. It's not really just you and your grandma, is it?" Alex asked. "I mean, your mom must be around fairly sometimes."

Emily saw her mom as a back, straight and narrow with a checkered jacket.

"She really isn't, Alex."

"Why?" Alex asked.

"I don't know," Emily said.

"Em?" Alex was looking at her in a way that made her think that maybe he was going to really talk to her now, really fill things in.

"Party in the bathroom?" Justin appeared in the open doorway, carrying two bottles of beer in each hand.

"Got to start it somewhere," Alex said.

Justin seemed satisfied with that.

Alex pushed himself up from the ground. He reached down and helped Emily up. Her legs were damp from the bathmat.

"Come on," Justin said. He backed out of the bathroom and switched off the light. "We're down the hall."

They turned from the main hallway toward the back of the house where the music was coming from. Justin led them into a small room.

Three guys all had their eyes glued to the TV. Justin kicked out a cord when he crossed the room, and one of the guys holding a controller looked up like he had just been pulled out from wherever he had been. Emily could see that Justin had detached the cord connecting the video game controller with the console. He dropped it, now useless, and leaned back into the couch. The game on the TV paused but the music kept playing.

"What's that for?" asked a guy with blond hair and a black sweater. Emily blushed when she realized he was staring at the curling iron she held in her hand. She tucked it at her side.

"This is Alex, my cousin," Justin said. "And his friend Emily."

"Hey, Emily," said someone else.

She wanted to back out through the door and not come back. But then the boy smiled and shrugged his shoulders. "I'm Tyler," he said. He had black hair and heavy dark eyebrows.

"Hi," she said.

"That's Steve and Mark," Justin said, jerking his thumb at the blond-haired guy on the floor and a stout, thick one rocking so hard on a reclining chair that it looked like the seat was going to snap off.

He turned back to the television and started talking to the guy named Mark. Emily felt stuck in place, not sure whether to go all the way into the room or to go all the way out. She backed her feet through the carpet and felt static collecting on the bottoms of her tights. She couldn't imagine having not stayed with Lucy and Alex, but right now, feeling uncomfortable and self-conscious at the party, she wished she were home. If she had known this was where they would end up, she might have stayed there when she had the chance.

"You want to sit down?" Tyler asked, his hand resting on the cushion beside him.

"I should find Lucy," she said to Alex.

"She'll come up and find you," Alex said.

"You think?"

"Yeah."

Emily left Alex at the door and stepped through the

bodies, cords, and food like she was navigating an obstacle course. She sat down next to Tyler on the couch and dropped the curling iron on the carpet. Alex looked distractedly out the door but he didn't make a move for the hallway. Eventually, he sat down on the floor with his back against the wall, his knees pulled up so they formed a triangle.

Of everything that had happened so far that night, this was the least comfortable. She and Alex were in the same room but far apart, and Lucy was somewhere downstairs, far away from both of them. When Emily felt most like the night was working, it was when she, Lucy, and Alex were in the same place, the same room, the same car, easy and comfortable. She wanted it to be the three of them again. She worried what would happen to Alex as the night went on.

Emily sank back into the couch. Tyler knocked her knee with his and pointed to the video game resuming on the TV. He gestured with the controller but he wasn't playing.

"You play?" he asked.

"No," Emily said, shaking her head.

"You want to?"

"Not really."

"You know Justin, right?"

"I know he's Alex and Lucy's cousin, but that's about all, really."

"You hear that sound?" Tyler asked. It was hard to hear anything over the TV, but Emily could feel, more than hear, something downstairs.

"What it is?"

"That," Tyler said, "is the sound of everyone who knows Justin."

Emily listened. There was the thump of the door and the clumping of boots on carpet. The house was filling up. "I hear he's pretty popular."

"That's one way of putting it."

Tyler's knee was still touching hers.

"I'm going to get a drink. You want one?"

Emily looked at Alex sitting by the door. She felt like she should stay where he was, but Tyler was already standing. Her knee felt like someone had taken a chunk of it right out, like it had stuck to Tyler's and was walking away without her.

"I'll come with you," she said.

Alex looked up when she left but he looked at her through eyes that didn't seem focused enough to see.

"I'm going down to the kitchen. Do you want anything?" she asked.

"I'm okay," Alex said.

Tyler knew his way around the house. He led her down a different hallway than the one she'd come through before and they ended up in the kitchen by using a narrow back staircase.

They weren't the only people in there. It was cold on the main floor and Emily wondered if the front door had been left open to facilitate the easy movement of people coming into the house.

Tyler shouldered past two people standing by the fridge, opened it, and took out two beers. He handed one to Emily and leaned against the counter. His jeans were tight and his socks were falling off his heels.

"So are you from here? I mean, I've met Justin's cousins a couple of times before, but you're new."

"I just met them, actually. Just a few hours ago."

"No way," Tyler said.

"I met Alex at the hospital and went with him to meet Lucy. We've just been driving around."

"It sucks a lot about Alex," Tyler said. "When Justin first found out, he wasn't doing great. I know he goes to the hospital to visit a lot."

"I didn't even know Alex had cancer," Emily said. "He didn't tell me until a little while ago."

"I guess it's not really something you just throw out there," Tyler said.

Emily hadn't thought of it like that. She had thought of it like they hadn't told her because she didn't need to know, because at the end of the night, she'd just drive home and everything would be encapsulated in that one single night.

"I guess not," she said.

"If you're not tied to them all night, come and find me," Tyler said. "My car's out front. We can just hang out or go for a drive or go somewhere else. We can figure out something to do."

The kitchen was getting crowded and Emily almost wanted to say yes, if only to get out of the house.

"Later?" she said, too much like a promise and not enough like she didn't care.

"I'll remember that." He leaned in so close that Emily smelled his breath, sticky and bitter. "You're really beautiful, you know."

Emily blushed and her face was hot and Tyler's breath was hot and she couldn't tell which was which.

"Emily?"

Lucy stood in the entrance to the kitchen looking like she was trying very hard to figure Emily out.

Emily backed away so fast she bumped into the counter behind her.

Tyler took a sip from his beer and gestured to the staircase with the bottle. "I'm heading up," he said. "I'll see you later?"

Emily watched him leave. She had a feeling that, beside her, Lucy was watching *her* watch him leave.

"Who's that?" Lucy asked.

"He's one of your cousin's friends."

"Justin has bad taste in friends," Lucy said.

"He doesn't seem too bad."

Lucy shrugged. "You haven't known him very long then, right?"

"I guess."

"So?" Lucy said. "Are you going to curl my hair?"

"I left the curling iron upstairs."

"Do you want to go get it?"

"And Alex?"

Lucy looked at her funny.

"You can get him, too."

chapter*twenty-two*

Lucy let Emily go up the stairs before her.

"I'll be right there, okay?" she said. "I just need to do something first."

"Okay. I'll see you in a minute."

Lucy went into the office on the main floor, shut the door, and sat on the leather couch. Her knees crept into her chest. She was trying to stop herself from doing something stupid, like she had the night of the dance. Her arms were tight around her legs. It helped. She could hold her entire body together with just her arms.

Emily and Alex were upstairs. Maybe he'd tell her now. She hoped he would. Then she could go up, take his hand, and rescue him from this night that had made his sickness worse than it had ever been before. One of the reasons she wasn't with him now herself was because she couldn't stop crying. The other reason was because she wanted him and Emily to have that moment. Alex wanted Lucy to be there, too, but Lucy wondered if maybe he'd be better at doing it than she was. Still, she wanted it over. She wanted the night to stop and for Alex to be safe.

Lucy wiped her eyes and checked her reflection in the mirror on the wall. Her brother was doing this night the way he was because it was the last New Year's Eve when he could do anything he wanted to. More than that, it might be the last night he could do something like this. But he was doing it for her, too. He was doing it because he didn't want her to be alone. Lucy stood up and walked to the door. She went upstairs to find her brother.

chapter*twenty-three*

Alex stayed in the room with his legs stretched out in front of him. He'd met Justin's friends before, once or twice when he'd stopped by with his mom or his dad for a visit. Alex thought they were mostly okay guys. He watched Emily leave the room with one of them, but he couldn't move. His legs had gone as heavy as lead. He wanted to follow her, but he couldn't.

The plan had been easy. They had designed it in stages. Find out when Emily would be at the hospital; wait until New Year's; take her to the restaurant; and meet up with Lucy. Get to know Emily a bit and then tell her.

Getting to know Emily was as far as they got. Telling her what they had to, Alex was finding out, was the hard part. But he had to do it.

Alex got up off the carpeted floor in the small room on the top floor of Justin's house.

"Hey, man, you leaving?"

"I'm just going to find my sister," Alex said. "See you later."

He had put it off for too long. It was time.

chapter*twenty-four*

Emily plugged the curling iron into an outlet by Justin's bed. Lucy sat on the floor. Alex lay beside them, his eyes closed. It was past the time when Emily could ask him if he was okay. He was not okay, but there wasn't anything she could do to help.

"Alex, watch carefully," Lucy said. "Open your eyes."

Emily was watching their exchanges more closely now, trying to pick apart the thing that they talked around in large voices and gestures.

Lucy turned to Emily and said, "Don't burn me, okay?"

"I won't." Emily held up the curling iron and snapped it open and closed a few times. Steam rose from the long blonde hair that had been left behind, melded to the metal.

She set the curling iron down on the bedside table and turned to Alex. He had a thin trickle of blood coming from his nose.

"Alex," she said. "Your nose is bleeding."

As if resigned to the increase in nosebleeds, Alex reached into his pocket and pulled out the Kleenex, already stained with dried blood from earlier. He held it up to his nose and leaned his head back.

Emily shut her eyes and when she did, she felt like she was spinning. She was tired. Remembering all the places she had been today was exhausting. She wanted to keep her eyes shut like that for the rest of the night. When she opened them, Alex was calmly trying to stop the nosebleed.

"Your hair's such a nice color," Emily told Lucy.

"Kind of."

"It is."

"What about mine?" Alex asked, smiling. His words were cloudy beneath the Kleenex and the sound made Emily turn around. Lucy was watching her brother carefully, but she didn't say anything about the nosebleed.

"What about chemotherapy?" Emily asked him. "I thought that was supposed to make you lose your hair."

"It does. It just grew back. It wasn't working in the end and they stopped the treatments." He ran his hand through his hair. "Looks good, right?"

Emily worked through one layer of Lucy's hair and then another. Eventually Alex balled up the Kleenex, wiped his finger under his nose, and sat up a little bit straighter.

"This is actually kind of fun, in a weird way," Lucy said.

"Yeah," Emily agreed.

Emily's cell phone rang. It was the wrong moment to interrupt.

"You'd think she'd get the hint that I don't want to talk to her," Emily said. "But she never does. If you guys knew my mom, you'd think she was crazy."

"Maybe not," Alex said.

"I mean, because what if we did know your mom?" Lucy said.

Alex leaned forward and Lucy looked over her shoulder. They were both looking at Emily.

"She'd have to be in town more often for you to know her."

"Maybe," Alex said. "But what if, instead, we just kind of know *of* her?"

"I don't know how you would," Emily said.

There was a knock on the door. It creaked open and there was a girl standing in the hall.

"Steph, you're here," Alex said.

Emily looked at the girl and then back at the top of Lucy's head. Once again, she felt like she did not belong here. Like she was back to being the person on the edge while everyone else knew what it meant to be at the center. Even when what came before seemed to belong to Emily, she was still new to Alex and Lucy.

"Yeah," Stephanie said. "Lucy said Justin was having a party. I thought you might be around." She inched into the room but didn't close the door. "Can we talk? Alex?"

Alex and Lucy exchanged a look and Emily continued

wrapping hair around and around the curling iron.

"Okay," Alex went to the door. He looked at his sister and then at Emily for so long and so hard that Emily knew that something had been going to happen and now maybe it wouldn't.

They left the room. The door clicked shut behind them.

"That's Stephanie," Lucy said after a minute. "I thought it would be different. She just picked the wrong time to come in, I think."

"You and Alex. Talking about my mom. That's a joke, right?"

Lucy didn't answer.

Emily set the curling iron to the side and dropped her hands into her lap. "Lucy?"

"We should wait for Alex to get back. This was his idea."

"What was his idea?"

"Tonight. Finding you at the hospital."

Emily felt like her forehead was on fire, growing hot enough that she was sweating in places that didn't usually sweat. Behind her ears. Her hairline. The space behind her knees.

"Finding me at the hospital? How did you know I'd be there?"

"Wait for Alex," she said. It was much quieter.

"I don't think I want to." Emily moved so she was sitting beside Lucy, staring at the side of her head because Lucy would not turn. "And how did he bring me here? We met at the hospital. I was visiting my grandmother and he said he was visiting a friend. He wasn't, but still, it was a coincidence."

"I think we should wait for him to get back." Lucy's voice was so low it was like a cement truck rolling over asphalt, packing it down.

Finally, Lucy looked at her.

"You knew I'd be there," Emily said. "You knew me before I knew you."

"Not exactly," Lucy said.

Downstairs there was yelling and music, and it sunk into Emily's head like an ache.

"Why is he here? Why am I here?"

Lucy's eyes were glassy, shiny when she answered.

"Alex left the hospital because we needed to find you."

"Me?" Emily asked. "Why?"

Lucy smiled crookedly, her lips going up at the corner.

"You know how sometimes there are secrets and they get covered up? And the only people who know about them end up being strangers, because they're too important to tell to the people they mean something to?"

"No," Emily said. "I don't."

"Me and Alex are strangers to you," Lucy said. "Or we were, anyway. And we know your secret."

Emily shook her head, not understanding. Lucy stared at her hands. When she looked back up, Emily could feel the change in the room.

"Emily," Lucy said, "you're our half-sister."

The smell of burning hair came from the too-hot curling iron. Emily leaned over and unplugged it from the wall. And then she left the room.

Alex and Stephanie were standing right outside the door.

"Em, come back," Lucy said, swinging her legs off the bed. Alex looked at her with eyes wide open and confused.

"You should've told me," Emily said to him.

He looked into the bedroom. Lucy was stumbling out. Her hair was half-curled and half-straight. Stephanie stood by the door, watching all three of them. Emily shouldered past her and tried to find the stairs.

"Emily, wait," Alex said.

"You should be in the hospital."

He looked from Emily to Lucy.

"I had to tell her," Lucy said.

Alex followed Emily down the hallway. The closer they got to the stairs the more people were in the way. Emily made the mistake of hesitating at the top of the stairs and when she did, Alex caught up to her.

"Please, don't," he said.

"This was planned? Meeting me at the hospital and taking me out here to tell me I'm related to you?"

Alex sighed and rubbed his forehead.

"Your mom and my dad," he said. "It happened when she was still in high school. They were together."

"*Together*," Emily said.

"He had been with my mom before that. Mine and Lucy's. It got complicated."

"How do you *know* this? How do you know and I don't?"

"Your mom started calling our house. She was looking for our dad."

"My mom?"

Emily pushed through the people at the top of the stairs and hurried to the main floor. She was walking so fast that she ran straight into Tyler. She could smell his deodorant through his shirt.

"Whoa. Where're you going?"

She looked behind her and Alex was still at the top of the stairs, trying to find his way through. She felt her stomach drop. He had known everything about her. All the hours they had spent together and he hadn't even tried to let her know. If he could keep the fact that they were half-siblings hidden, there might be more that he hadn't shared.

"To find you," Emily said to Tyler. "So we can go somewhere. You said your car's out front."

"Yeah," Tyler nodded his head. "That sounds good."

Emily stuck her hand into his. It was damp and warm and it swallowed hers up whole.

chapter*twenty-five*

Lucy didn't know how it had happened. She wanted to take it all back, wipe the entire night clean and start again. A choose-your-own adventure. She'd know the pages to avoid the next time.

She was the one who had solved the mystery of the phone calls. She had found out about Emily.

She had been home with her dad all morning on Christmas Eve. She was helping wrap a present for her mom. It was a gold necklace in a blue cardboard box. She pulled the edges of the wrapping paper tight against the corners of the box and taped on a bow. Lucy thought she was probably the worst gift wrapper out of all the members of her family. She couldn't get the hang of taping the sides down before the paper billowed and created a pocket of extra wrapping in the middle. She knew the rest of them could guess at the presents she had wrapped because of her unfortunate technique.

"What do you think?" she asked, holding up the wrapped necklace.

"Looks good, kid," her dad said.

"You're not even looking."

"Lucy, it's great," he said, taking the gift and placing it under the tree. "It doesn't have to be professional. We just have to get these things wrapped before your mom gets home."

"Mom's going to wish they were neater."

"No, she's not."

Lucy was sitting by her dad, taping hastily, when the phone rang. Without even thinking about it, she let her dad answer the phone while she watched TV and wrapped. Ten minutes later, she realized he was still gone.

Alex had told her about the phone calls that came to the house every day. Lucy hadn't picked one up yet because she was in school. She wondered if this call was one of those.

Her dad wasn't in the kitchen or the dining room or in the office on the main floor. The rooms upstairs were empty. She finally heard the sound of the bathroom ventilation fan. Through the door, she listened to the indecipherable words he was saying in a private conversation she wasn't allowed to be a part of. She was still standing there when her dad came out of the bathroom with the portable phone in his hand.

"You okay?" he asked.

"Who is she?" Lucy asked him.

"Who's who?"

"The woman you were talking to. She's been calling here for the last two weeks. Every day. Alex got the first phone call."

"Neither of you told me," he said.

"Yeah, well, it was weird. She didn't leave a message. She didn't want you to call her."

"I know," her dad said. "I know."

"Alex thinks he might've figured out who she is. Or he found someone who might know."

Her dad's face made Lucy almost wish she hadn't said anything. His forehead wrinkled, creases building from the bridge of his nose to his hairline.

"Lucy," he said, "I think I'll need you to explain this from the beginning."

"There isn't really a beginning. Alex got the phone calls. He went into the hospital and heard the same woman in the cafeteria. He figured out she was visiting this old woman in geriatrics. I think he wants to go up there and ask her about it."

"Why is he so interested?"

"Come on, Dad," Lucy said. "Some woman we don't know has been calling our house for a couple of weeks, looking for you. Why's she looking for you?"

He sighed and passed the phone from one hand to the other.

"Let's go downstairs," he said.

She followed her dad into the kitchen. There was half a pot of coffee left over from breakfast. Her dad poured it into a used mug, the coffee stains thick up the sides. He added a couple of teaspoons of sugar. Lucy's mom and dad drank their coffee the same way. Their mugs were interchangeable.

"Do you want anything?" her dad asked.

"Dad? This is weird. Why aren't you just telling me what's going on?"

"I am," he said. "I am."

He pulled a plastic container out of the cupboard. Lucy's aunt had baked cookies and squares and packaged them up for Christmas. She really got into the spirit of holidays. Her son, Justin, didn't get into holidays. He just got excited when his parents left home to go traveling during them so he had the big house to himself. He had called Lucy to tell her he was having a party there on New Year's Eve. She didn't know if she'd go.

Her dad set the container on the table and pulled out the chair. Lucy sat across from him. She took a shortbread cookie and picked at the candied cherries sticking out of the top.

"The name of the woman who has been calling is Kate Henderson," her dad said. "The woman your brother's probably seen is her mother. She's in long-term care at the hospital."

"So she's like Alex."

Her dad flinched at that. His shoulders bowed and his head nodded. "In a way."

"How do you know her?" Lucy asked.

"I knew her when she was in high school," he said.

"So she was your friend or something?"

He rubbed at his head. "It's complicated, Lucy."

"Stop being weird. Why won't you just tell me?"

"Look," he said, "there's someone who needs to know all of this but right now, I'm not sure if that's you."

"Know what? I have no idea what you're talking about," Lucy said, frustration thick and heavy. "Is it something Mom doesn't even know?"

"Your mother knows," he said and sighed. "I dated Kate Henderson when she was in high school. I was in college."

"But you knew Mom in college. I thought you guys dated all through college."

"She broke up with me, kid," he said, making a crooked smile. "I went home for the summer and I met Kate."

The way her dad described the summer was in footnotes and abbreviations. But it seemed he met Kate at a diner that was still in downtown Victoria. The diner was bright with red-painted walls. It was black-and-white checkered floors and wide, clean windows, and blinds rolled up to the ceiling. It was the sun setting and night outside revealing the reflections of faces on the windows, and all of that possibility. It was steam and noise in the kitchen and plates sliding across metal counters, the waitresses who said,

"What can I get you, dear?" and the line cooks who said, "Order's up!" and people having conversations, and you know they're all interesting and fascinating and you wish you could sit at every table and be a part of everything. It was two burgers and fries and a milkshake, Kate's vanilla, her dad's chocolate; it was their straws, skinny and swapped; it was the twirling of flavors passed across the table. It was kissing later in the car; it was sweet and cool and summer.

"Dad," Lucy said. "I still don't get it."

"I know," he said. "I know."

He stopped and drank his coffee. When he spoke, his words were slow and even.

"At the time, I thought they balanced out. Your mom breaking up with me and Kate going out with me. The good things were on one side and the bad things on the other, and that was what love was, in the end, just this balancing act. And you start with the good things, the dates, the love, the togetherness, and to that collection you add the bad things, or you don't add them—someone else does—or it's a combination of where it comes from, from you or her or them."

"Sounds nice, Dad, but what does all that mean?"

"I got a phone call from Vancouver, where your mother was. She was pregnant."

"With Alex?"

"With Alex," he said, nodding.

"And Kate?"

"Kate was pregnant, too," he said.

It took Lucy a minute to understand. She imagined something in her head. It was like the diner. It took a moment to make it real in order to understand what had happened.

Her dad said, "Your mom had Alex. Kate had a girl named Emily."

"And she's your daughter?"

Her dad nodded.

Lucy shivered.

"Kate decided it would be best if I didn't meet Emily. And I had gone back to Vancouver to be with your mom and to keep up with college. So I thought it would be the easiest, too. But now Kate has changed her mind. She thinks that keeping me from meeting Emily was a mistake. Emily is almost eighteen now, like Alex. And Kate thinks it's time."

"Do you want to meet her?" Lucy asked.

"I do," her dad said. "I think it's the right thing to do."

Lucy picked at the shortbread cookie, but she didn't eat it. It sat on her plate, crumbling like sand in her fingers.

What it meant, the things her dad said, was that she had a half-sister. She and Alex had another sibling.

"With Alex in the hospital," Lucy's dad said, "I don't want to bring this up over Christmas. I don't want your mom to have to worry over the holidays. So I'm not going to see Emily until after the New Year. It might seem strange to you, to have this secret, but I need you to keep it for just a little longer. Can you do that?"

Lucy didn't know if she could, if she could promise her dad that she wouldn't tell Alex. He was in hospital and wasn't coming out. He needed to know there was another sibling in their family. He had to know there was somebody else. If anything happened and he didn't know that? Somehow it seemed that his not knowing made as big a hole as anything.

"I won't tell," she lied.

"Thank you," her dad said. He ate what was left of the cookie on her plate. She tapped her fingernails on the table and thought about what she was going to do next.

"We should finish wrapping the presents," she said. "Mom's probably going to be home soon."

"You go put something good on TV. I'll be right there."

"Okay," Lucy stood up, but stopped at the kitchen door. "Dad? I'd like to meet her, too. Emily."

"We'll see," he said. "We'll see how it goes."

Standing beside Alex at Justin's house, Lucy swallowed hard. She hoped Emily would come back. She needed Emily to come back.

chapter*twenty-six*

Alex couldn't believe he'd missed his chance to tell her. Stephanie was standing beside him at the top of the stairs and Lucy was gripping his arm.

"Oh my God, what do we do?" Lucy asked.

"I don't know. I don't even know what happened."

"It's my fault. I told her everything. It just came out."

Alex couldn't get angry. He couldn't even be frustrated. All he could do was put his arm around her shoulders.

"At least she knows," he said. "Now all we have to do is find her."

"Where do we even look?"

"I'll go check around the block. You stay here, in case she comes back."

"You can't go alone," Lucy said. "Alex, you know you're not doing great."

"I have to. It was stupid to wait," Alex said. "I'll be right back. I'll call you when I find her. Steph, I'm sorry."

"I'll see you when you get back," she said. "I'll stay with Lucy."

Alex's legs shook on the stairs. He gripped the banister. He could hardly stand. The only thing pushing him forward was the awful sense of regret in his chest.

Outside, it was colder than before. The damp chill reached into his chest and shook him from his bones. He stuffed his hands in his pockets and started walking.

Lucy had told him about Emily and explained it all while they sat in his hospital room, eating pumpkin pie the day after Christmas.

"We have to meet her," he had said, almost immediately. "And talk to her."

"Hang on. Dad said we have to keep it a secret. At least until after he tells Mom. And then when he finds Emily."

"But listen to this. She's our half-sister. We can meet her. Just me and you. She might like us."

"How are you going to do that from the hospital? "And what are you going to say? 'Oh, hey, our dad is also your dad so I guess that makes us siblings'? I think we have to listen to Dad on this one. This is his thing to do, not ours."

"You have to understand, I don't know how long I have," Alex said. "Dad might see her in a couple of days or a couple of weeks. But it could be a couple of months. I don't have that."

"I get that, but still."

"Think about it. I've been in here all month. I might not get another chance to leave. If we do it on New Year's, it could be my last time to get out of this place. I already know when she visits her grandmother. All we'd have to do is wait until she gets out and figure out a way to get her to come with us."

"What do you mean," Lucy said, pausing between each word, "your last chance to leave the hospital?" She said it so slowly.

"One more night," he said. "I need one more night to do something that really matters. New Year's Eve is the perfect time. And what better 'something' than finding Emily? We can meet her and we can tell her who we are."

"Okay, Alex? You've lost me. It is not a good idea for you to leave the hospital. There's a reason you're in here."

"Other people have done it," he said. "Other people go on these trips. They have cancer; they find out they don't have long, and they go out for one last night."

"And then they die!" Lucy said without thinking. Her hands were shaking. "It doesn't end good. It's not all happy endings."

"But it would be if we find her. If we meet Emily."

Alex stayed awake in the small hospital room after Lucy went home. He knew he had to find a way to get them in the same place, him, Lucy, and Emily. He didn't have time for his dad to figure out when he was going to meet Emily and

Kate. He didn't have time. And knowing about Emily, this girl who was his age exactly, released the hard pull he had on his heart. She could be someone for Lucy. She could be someone for Lucy when he was gone.

chapter*twenty-seven*

The missed-call notification was blinking on the screen of Emily's cell phone like a warning sign. Her mom had called twice while she was at Justin's house. She tucked it back into her pocket and followed Tyler to his car. It was parked around the corner and at the end of another long residential street.

Emily had never known who her father was, and now she had been handed an identity, or at least a name. No, more than that. Meeting Alex and Lucy made it so she had more than a dad. She had a family.

Part of her didn't believe it, but part of her was overwhelmingly certain it was true. Alex and his leukemia and his confinement to the hospital had allowed him to find her. It had allowed him and Lucy to take her somewhere on New Year's to tell her she was related to their family, and they shared the same father.

She couldn't understand why they hadn't told her from the start. Alex could have done it the second she was walking with him from the hospital or sitting with him in the restaurant or driving in the big van filled with the taxidermy animals. There were so many moments she could see that handful of words slipping out: "You're our half-sister." There had been so much time. Instead she had only just found out now.

But would she have gone with Alex if that was one of the first things he had said? If he had come up to her and told her that they were related before they'd spent time together and before she met Lucy and before they ended up here, she knew she wouldn't have gone with him. She would have just taken the bus home and she'd have never known.

Still, Emily couldn't go back into Justin's house. Not yet. She needed to think about what had happened.

Her phone vibrated again in her pocket. Her mom had never phoned her so often or so many times in a row. It had started when she left the hospital with Alex. She wondered if Alex's father—*her* father—had contacted her mom and let her know that Emily might have found something out.

Emily wished there had been a, 'When you turn eighteen, I'll tell you everything, but I want to wait until you're ready.' She was ready at six. She was ready at twelve. And if she wasn't living with her mother, why couldn't she live with her father? She was ready, at seventeen, to know everything.

Now that she knew who he was, Emily wasn't sure what she was going to do. She would have to go back to Justin's and find Alex and Lucy. They could help her figure things out.

Tyler left the keys hanging in the ignition of the car. There weren't streetlights down the stretch of street where he'd parked. Even the backlight of the odometer faded into black. Emily couldn't see her hand in front of her face. She felt Tyler sitting beside her in the driver's seat.

"You want a beer?" Tyler asked, reaching into the backseat. Emily heard the sound of cardboard tearing.

Emily's hands were resting on her thighs. She couldn't make sense of all the thoughts she was trying to hold still in her head. She had a half-sister. She had a half-brother. She had always had them, but she hadn't known it. Now she was going to lose Alex before she ever really knew him. "Sure."

Tyler popped the top of her can and she took a sip.

"Good night so far?" he asked her.

"It's been a long night." She twisted her fingers together on her lap until Tyler separated them and held her hand.

"It's New Year's," he said.

"I know."

"You guys did a lot before you came here?"

"Yeah, we did," Emily said.

"There's still a lot we can do. It's not even midnight yet."

"Almost," she said.

"Em, you want to get out of here?" he asked.

"I don't know. Not yet."

Tyler reached his arm around her shoulders and it settled down too tight. He pulled her in and put her off balance and she slipped on the seat. Her cheek hit his shoulder. She didn't want to breathe normally, because it felt wrong to do it against his chest. She took careful, shallow breaths that sat near her throat. Her eyes were wet, but they weren't crying. Everything concentrated and settled in her throat, a knot of knowing and not knowing, and not knowing what to say.

"Hey," he said, putting his hand on the side of her cheek. "What's wrong? I thought we were having fun."

"We are."

"We could be having more fun."

She saw his face coming closer. His eyes were closed and his lips, eyelids, and nose coming toward her seemed so huge that she felt a sick, queasy feeling in her stomach. She hadn't meant to be here. She had just needed to get out of the house. And now she was stuck. Tyler's mouth was wet and open. It was this big, great black hole swallowing her up. It pushed sweat down the back of her neck.

"Look, I'm sorry," she said suddenly, but she was talking into Tyler's mouth. "I don't want to do this."

"Yes, you do."

She felt his words in her teeth and on her tongue, hot and uncomfortable.

"I want to go back to Justin's."

Tyler's chest pressed up against hers when he moved

their bodies on the seats. Emily's back pressed up against the passenger window.

"Stop," she said. "I need to get back to Justin's." She pushed on his arms but they didn't move. It scared her that she couldn't make him move.

"No, you don't."

The pressing of lips. It wasn't soft or careful, it was everywhere, until Emily forgot where she was. And then, in the dark, she found her thighs and her feet, her elbows and her shoulders. From beneath Tyler, they connected like a picture, drawing itself together line by line until she was aware of her strength again.

"Tyler, stop." She pushed against him with everything.

He pulled his face away. In the dark, she could see the outlines of the hollowed places in his cheeks, beneath his chin.

"I could do anything," he said. "No one would know."

"I would," Emily said quietly. He was still pressing against her. She could feel his thighs, tensing like he wasn't even trying. "You would."

His hand was tight around her wrist. She didn't know when it had moved there, the knuckle of his thumb paler than anything from the pressure. Her wrist bone felt like it was slipping out from the place it was supposed to be and her skin was stretching. Tyler saw her looking at her arm and he looked at his hand that held it.

"Let go," she said.

Tyler did. He let her go and she pulled her hand into her chest. She could still feel the weight of him, but it wasn't a heavy weight. It didn't scare her.

She inched her back up the seat, sliding her legs from between his until they were hers again. Her hair fell down the back of her jacket. It fell down her collar and made her shiver.

Tyler didn't move, but she could feel him looking at her, just as carefully as he had looked at his hand holding her wrist. Emily pulled at her hair and combed it straight again with her fingers, finding something to do with her hands so she didn't have to look at him.

"I'm leaving," Emily said. Her voice didn't sound like she remembered it. It sounded like it came from somewhere that wasn't quite her throat, not from vocal chords that were familiar. It was like walking into a room with speakers placed far away from one another, when the music didn't come from where you expected it to, and it sounded strange.

She unlocked the car door and slammed it shut. She started walking. She couldn't remember the direction they had come from, but she had to get away from Tyler's car. She hoped she had chosen right and that the street she was on would take her back to Justin's house.

She could still feel the hole left behind in her lungs from the way Tyler's ribs carved out space from her chest. She crossed her arms in front of her like she could keep everything inside. She was lost in the maze of suburban homes, built close together and tightly cemented.

"Em!"

It was Alex, sick and outside and alone. She turned around and waited for him to catch up.

"Em, I'm sorry," he said. He looked like he had been outside for a long time. He didn't have a jacket on. That made it worse. There was too much space inside her chest and she didn't want to fill it with Alex, even though he was her brother. After what had almost happened with Tyler, she wanted to fill it with herself and she couldn't get hold of that yet.

"You didn't do anything to say sorry for," she said.

"I should've told you right away what was going on. I just, I didn't want you to get freaked out and not come with us. Me and Lucy wanted to meet you. And we wanted you to like us."

"When did you find out about me?" she asked.

"Christmas."

"Oh." It was so recent. There was so much she wanted to know, but she felt too tired to ask.

"Where's Lucy?"

"She stayed at the house, in case you came back. She was going to call me if you did."

"She let you go out here by yourself?"

Alex hesitated. "Em, Lucy wants to get me back to the hospital."

"I want that, too," Emily said.

"I needed to find you."

"You did," Emily said. "But we should go back."

"I know."

Emily held him tight around the shoulders. Their legs matched step for step, lining up like they had hours before in the hospital atrium, but more slowly now.

Alex made a sound that Emily thought was a sigh, but he was bent over double, holding his stomach. He groaned.

"Alex?"

He didn't even lift his head.

"Alex? What's happening?"

He collapsed on the ground. His legs crept up into his stomach and he became very still.

"Alex?" Emily kneeled next to him on the cement. They were beside a row of houses, the lights inside off and the outsides quiet. Emily held Alex's shoulder. She leaned over and held his hand. She held on and on.

chapter*twenty–eight*

"I called for an ambulance," Emily said.

She had helped Alex move from the cement to the grass and then called the hospital. She called Lucy, but she didn't pick up.

"This is good," Alex said.

"You feel better?"

"Yeah, but the ground is cold."

Hesitantly, self-consciously, Emily positioned herself on the cold grass beside him, their sides pressed up together, sharing body heat.

In the sky, the constellations seemed to form and re-form even though they were meant to be immutable. Emily found the Big Dipper and it looked like how she drew boxy geometric shapes on graph paper in school. She wondered if Alex, lying on the grass beside her, was seeing this same constellation in the exact same way, or if it was something completely different to him.

How differently from before, she saw Alex now. A *brother*.

Her family wasn't only her and her grandmother, and sometimes her mother. And it wasn't even just Alex. There was Lucy now, too. Lucy with her coat with the fur hood and high boots and the way she talked like she could tell you anything.

She had gained a brother and a sister in just one night.

"Alex?"

He didn't answer. His chest went up and down, but the seconds between breaths seemed like too many.

She didn't like the quiet at the end of things, when she wanted the space inside her to fill up with everything she still had to say to him, everything they had missed or wouldn't have. Her chest ached as she looked up at the stars and saw how they spread out in every single direction, like they went on forever.

Emily looked at Alex, lying beside her, the damp grass cushioning his shoulders. No matter how well she had come to know him tonight, she could never know everything she wanted to.

Alex was going to die, but it wouldn't just be him disappearing. When someone dies, Emily thought, you lose a world. And they hadn't had enough time. They didn't have growing up with someone and years of memories to go back to. They had one night that started in an elevator and ended a few hours later in a neighborhood on the other side of the city. What was happening now was something she couldn't stop. And all of those pamphlets from before, the typed pages of instructions, they didn't explain this. They couldn't say what it was like to lose someone you loved without having had any time to love them.

When Emily tipped her head back, the sky looked different. She thought at first that stars were sliding down out of the sky. Small white lights falling down.

"Hey," Emily whispered. "I think it's snowing."

Alex raised his hand, palm up. A smattering of flakes landed on his open hand. He closed his fingers around them and placed his arm at his side.

"Tell me a story, Em," he said.

Her back was cold where she felt the soggy grass through the material of her jacket. "What about?" She blinked at the snowflakes falling on her face.

"Tell me what you remember about being five."

"Why five?" she asked.

Alex looked at her, his head sliding to the side and his cheek pressing into the grass. "I like five." He smiled. "I didn't have cancer when I was five."

"How old was Lucy?"

"Three. You're lucky we waited to find you. You definitely wouldn't have liked Lucy when she was three."

"I think I probably would have," she said.

They were quiet again, but Emily was thinking. She could

feel Alex looking at her and she closed her eyes tight. She didn't remember what five was, but she had feelings that sat in her body trying to remind her.

"I remember being at daycare," Emily said finally. "It was in this old house in my neighborhood, with three stories and an attic and tall glass windows. I remember looking outside and it was raining. I was waiting for my grandma, wondering why it was taking her so long to pick me up." She squeezed her eyes shut tighter and used the pressure to scratch the itch out of her nose, the wrinkled creases doing the work of her fingers.

"When I was little, it didn't make sense to me how some-times days would go by so fast and other times it would be this awful stretch that I just wanted to be over. Now, when-ever it seems like the time is going really slowly, I see that window with the raindrops. Like I can see all of them, going so slow it makes my chest hurt."

Alex moved closer to her so that their sides were touch-ing from their shoulders to their calves, this soft weight that Emily wanted to concentrate on, wanted to hang on to. She bit down on the inside of her cheek.

"This night went so fast," Emily said. "I know it isn't really like that, but it's just the way everything happened, like I didn't even have time to think about it. Now I want it to slow down. Now that I know, I want more time."

Alex didn't say anything and she hated the quiet. His face was ghostly white in the darkness. She reached out and held his hand, a hand that didn't hold back.

"I remember being left alone a lot," Emily continued. *Just keep talking*, she thought, because if she was talking, it had to mean that Alex was listening. "My mom was gone and my grandparents were still working until I started elementary school. I used to wish so hard for there to be someone else out there, like a secret sister or a twin or a best friend that I'd meet and that I wouldn't have to worry about losing. And I wouldn't have to worry about being alone. But there wasn't anyone else. There was just me and I got used to that. And it's a good thing to get used to. Or I always thought it was. Making it easy to be alone because it was the only real thing."

"It's not."

"But that's how I felt," Emily said.

She had a pricking feeling, like needles under her skin, like a shiver set deep in her spine. Alex was going to be alone. It didn't matter how fast or slow time was going now, she couldn't stop it, pinch it between her fingers and make it still. At the end of that, there was going to be a loneliness that didn't have an ending.

"Do you want to know what I remember about being five?" Alex asked.

"What do you remember?"

She didn't know how long went by without Alex answering. She turned her head to look at him. The damp grass pressed against her cheek. His face was pale and the night had left two inky thumbprints under his eyes. Emily's eyes pricked from behind and she blinked them closed.

After a long moment, Emily turned her head back toward the sky and she searched the night for the constellations she knew would always be there.

Her cell phone rang. This time it was Lucy calling.

Emily answered the phone and told her sister where to find them.

Acknowledgments

This book couldn't have been written without the kind advice and thoughtful support of many people. I owe so many thanks to Richard Dionne and Peter Carver at Red Deer Press for placing my book on their publishing list, and to my editor, Kathy Stinson, whose picture book, *Red Is Best*, I've had on my bookshelf for years. I want to thank Deborah Wills, my English and Creative Writing professor at Mount Allison University, for agreeing to supervise a creative writing project, and reading and commenting on the additions and revisions that ultimately grew into this book. And then to Karen Bamford and Janine Rogers for both reading this manuscript and encouraging me to try to get it published. I also have to include Lachlan and Naoko, James, Bob, Lynne, and Mark at Rags of Time Bookstore in Sackville, New Brunswick, for their encouragement and support and conversation. Finally to my parents for always supporting writing and placing it above everything else, and to my sister because, let's face it, this one is for her.

Photo credit: Erin Bright

An Interview with the Author

1. What inspired you to write this story?
Before We Go started with the idea of two teenagers leaving a hospital together on New Year's Eve. I wanted to write about something that happened in a short amount of time. Just a few hours in one night. I wanted to see what would happen.

In my first draft, Alex didn't have cancer and Emily wasn't visiting her grandmother. They met and spent New Year's Eve together. They went to a lot of restaurants. They found a camera. They solved a mystery. They broke into a library. But that first draft didn't really work. Until they had the connection—that they were related—the urgency of their time together wasn't there. I'm not saying that two teenagers can't just spend a New Year's Eve together, but that underlying connection let me explore their past as well as all of the events that happen in one single night.

Alex and Emily drew me into their separate worlds. Emily's loneliness was overwhelming for me to write about, along with Alex's feeling of having no way out of his situation. I was interested in how a complex and important relationship could be hindered and transformed when time was an issue. The idea that relationships grow over weeks and months and years was reversed. Setting a time limit on how long they could know each other changed everything. I wanted to write a book where these two characters faced an obstacle to extending their relationship further, and explore how urgent one night could become because of it.

2. How did you come up with the title?

I saw Emily, Lucy, and Alex as three characters, each on very different paths. In a way, they were all "going" somewhere. For Alex, having cancer meant that he was not likely to survive. Emily's grandmother passing away would mean an entire new way of life for Emily, one that might involve staying in her grandmother's house, or possibly moving to Vancouver to be with her distant mother. And Lucy—I saw Lucy as on her own path, one that she couldn't even realize yet. Hers was something that was exciting, and she would have to be fearless and brave.

All of these characters were going somewhere but, before they did, I wanted to see what happened when they had one last night together. The title comes from this shared night, before everything changes, and they each move on to the next part of their lives.

3. Your blog has an interesting title, too. How did you come up with that one?

I write *Girl to the Rescue* (http://girltotherescue.blogspot. com/), a literary blog that reviews mostly young adult literature, children's books, graphic novels, and fantasy, which are really some of my favorite genres. I started *Girl to the Rescue* after I finished my MA in English as a way to get back to reading young adult literature and fantasy, two categories strangely lacking in both my undergrad and graduate school classes.

The title comes from Bruce Lansky's *Girls to the Rescue* series, published in the 1990s. By happy coincidence, Lansky was one of the first authors that I met when I was younger, and one of the first authors that I actually wanted to meet. His collections of short stories rewrote fairy tales, folk tales, and contemporary stories to feature a female heroine in the place of a Prince Charming. The books were written for children and adolescents, and I think I started to read them when I was around eight or nine.

Lansky's short story in the first *Girls to the Rescue* book, "The Fairy Godmother's Assistant," was about a young girl who apprentices with the local fairy godmother. She was this incredibly capable character who doled out advice to Cinderella, two princes, and a king. Although the title of my blog comes from those books, I like to think of it as a sort of coming-to-the-rescue of readers looking for recommendations for some really great books.

4. *Before We Go* is your first novel. What other writing have you done?

I have been writing for as long as I can remember. Recently, a lot of my writing has fallen under "papers for English university courses," which includes writing *about* books, but not actually writing books myself—and short stories because they wrap up a lot quicker than novels. But mostly, I like to write books for young adults. What this really means is that I start with a character or a story, then write, write, write, save the document, and move onto another one. It's a really bad habit, but as soon as I finish one draft, I'm already being pulled into another story. As a result, I have a folder of these unedited, first-draft manuscripts on my computer. *Before We Go* is the first one that I actually went farther with when I tumbled into the painstaking job of revising and editing.

Young adult literature is my favorite genre to read and write, but I would really like to write a fantasy novel. So far I have a few ideas, but I haven't written anything yet!

5. Did writing your screenplay (and placing second in a screenwriting contest for it) have any impact on the writing of your novel?

I was lucky enough to go to an undergraduate university (Mount Allison University in New Brunswick) that was very supportive of creative projects undertaken by students. When I was writing the most during university, I wrote a manuscript (unedited!) called *Mack and Tripp*. It was a mystery story but alternated between the perspectives of two characters. Each character had different "clues" regarding the mystery, and the better they got to know each other, the more the mystery began to unwind and, in consequence, affect their relationship.

At the same time, I was getting very interested in screenwriting. In a complicated series of emails from "a friend of a friend of a friend," I was sent a screenplay to edit, and this was the first time I had actually seen what one looked like. I was also watching a TV show called *Veronica Mars*, which had been created and written by Rob Thomas, who I was familiar with because of the books that he wrote for young adults (including *Rats Saw God*). I started to think about the connection between writing and screenwriting, and since I had finished writing a manuscript, I decided to try it out. The reason I believe I was fortunate to attend Mount Allison University, is because I was able to apply for funding for this project, and so I spent four months in the summer between my third and fourth year of university adapting my manuscript into a screenplay.

Knowing about the screenwriting process doesn't affect how I write now, but knowing that there is always the possibility of adaptation, and changing a finished manuscript into a screenplay later, leaves a side door open to going back to something that has already been written.

6. Have you always wanted to be a writer? Do you have any other professional ambitions?

I can't remember a time when I didn't want to be a writer. And for as long as I've been a writer, I've been a reader. I remember the best feeling about reading a book was being completely taken in by a set of characters, a setting, and a story. I would get roped in. The more I read, the more I realized that I didn't just want to be taken in by stories, I wanted to know how that happened, how a reader could be taken in by a story. I realized the way you find that out is through writing yourself.

Most of the jobs that I've had so far have to do, in some way, with books, reading, or writing. I've reviewed books for newspapers and publishing companies; I've edited books for children and young adults; I've worked as a research assistant for English professors; and I've worked for literary journals.

My favorite job that I've had so far was working at a second-hand bookstore during university. I am currently planning to get my PhD in English, because it creates a continuous opportunity to read and write. But any job that involves reading, writing, writing about reading, and reading about writing would be the best.

7. What are you working on now?
Right now, I am working on two projects.

The first one is editing and revising *Mack and Tripp*, the mystery story I mentioned earlier that is shared between two characters, and I'm trying to discover the best way to tell that story.

The second project is a book I started writing this summer. It is a young adult novel about a family that is completely changed when one of its own is sent to prison. It involves time travel, multiple universes, the World Wildlife Federation, and the secrets family members keep from one another. I'm currently three-quarters of the way through my first draft.